Refugees And Other Stories

Celu Amberstone

Kashallan Press, 2022

I0609815

This is a work of fiction. Similarities to real people, places, or events are entirely coincidental.

REFUGEES AND OTHER STORIES

First edition. August 31, 2022.

Copyright © 2022 Celu Amberstone.

ISBN: 978-1990581113

Written by Celu Amberstone.

Table of Contents

Foreword
by Dr Allan Weiss
associate professor of English and Humanities, York University

One of the hallmarks of twenty-first-century fantastic fiction in Canada and elsewhere is the growing diversity of voices working in the field. Writers from the Black, Indigenous, LGBTQ+, disabled, and other marginalized communities have come forth in increasing numbers, using the tropes of science fiction, fantasy, utopian/dystopian literature, and other fantastic genres to explore such themes as racism, sexism, colonialism, and exploitation. Many authors from these backgrounds have said that what is considered to be purely fantastic for dominant groups – alien invasion, alien abduction, and even the apocalypse – is historical reality for them.

Celu Amberstone has emerged as one of the key figures in this development in Canada. As an author of Scots-Irish and Cherokee heritage, she writes science fiction and fantasy tales that are deeply informed by elements of her European and Indigenous cultural roots. This collection of her shorter works, including one novella, deals with not only her own favourite themes but also those of other Indigenous authors. In her powerful stories, characters struggle with the problems of trying to reconcile various personal, family, and cultural identities.

Many of her protagonists find themselves torn between the demands of families and communities as they seek their own individual selves and how they fit into broader groups. For example, in "An Act of Power," Candace must find her grandmother's medicine bundle and where she fits into the Singing Wind Reservation's fight to protect the land against encroaching loggers. She is caught between family, represented by her grandmother, and political leaders and activists like the band council and her boyfriend Jonas. The bundle contains the power of her family's animal spirit, the cougar, and so she has to identify spiritually and quite literally with that animal. Fantasy – if we can fit the story into that genre, something that is not very clear-cut in this cultural context – gives Amberstone the opportunity to present in concrete ways what is most often a psychological and philosophical process. Fantastic fiction externalizes the internal, and so metamorphosis becomes the visible illustration of what is happening inside Candace. Much the same happens to Mara in "Guardians of the Bright Isles"; here, we see the other side of Amberstone's identity as Mara returns to Ireland to save the home of members of her own extended as well as immediate family: the water spirits living near and on Bright Island. The self in these stories is only one embodiment of a long line of a racial and family identity that dates back many centuries, if not millennia.

As one might expect of an Indigenous author, a major theme in Amberstone's work is colonialism. The title story is a fine example; as humanity has destroyed the environment of Earth, aliens come and "rescue" people from our dying planet. The story begins by portraying humanity's new home, Tallav'Wahir, as utopian, and the narrator, Qwalshina, is an Indigenous woman who does all she can to become one with the land on which she now lives. Newcomers from Earth like Sleek and Jim Talbot ("Jimtalbot") have a more difficult time adjusting, and indeed are obliged to surrender their pasts in order to live in what is now supposed to be their homes. As the story progresses, however, the "Benefactors" rules take on a more sinister air. Amberstone subtly draws a parallel between that destruction of the Earthlings' emotional, cultural, and other roots and what was done to Indigenous children in residential schools, where they were also required to give up their family and other backgrounds. In fact, the Benefactors, as the aliens want to be called, prove to be every bit as patronizing and condescending as the Canadian government and the various churches have been toward Indigenous peoples throughout the country's history.

The protagonist of "A Dragon's Price" is the native-born sex-slave of a conquered land. She has to make compromises to survive, but that comes at the cost of her dignity and her acceptance by her compatriots. Like the Europeans in North America, the story's invaders brought liquor – waskyja, an obvious parallel with whisky – to weaken and control the natives. Even her name, Red Bird Singing, calls up Indigenous echoes. She speaks to the invaders in a pidgin form of their language, and says not what she really thinks or feels but what they want to hear from her. Scholars have long remarked upon the sort of linguistic and physical masquerading that subordinate peoples have to engage in to function in a colonized society. The same pattern of paralleling and echoing appears in "Magic of Crimson." Shashil is an Indigenous adolescent woman living during the early days of European colonization. While on her spirit quest, she encounters a being from a parallel "mirroring" world that is experiencing its own alien invasion because of what is happening on Earth (or at least we assume Shashil's world is our own). She must make her own choices about how to do deal with her land's crisis and that of the Ani'Ya'Ron or "Seal People. Like so many of the other stories in the collection, "Magic of Crimson" confronts a young woman with the need to discover her own identity, and to choose her own path and way of fighting those who would deprive her and her people of their legacy.

Like these common themes, certain images and symbols recur throughout Amberstone's stories. For instance, her female characters possess and exert power through the feminine: their sexuality in "Guardians of the Bright Isles," "A Dragon's Price," the comical "Mother's New Sweetie," and "Magic of Crimson," and menstrual blood in the latter story. Water spirits appear in the novella and "Magic of Crimson," in one form or another, while animals play a significant role in nearly all the stories, whether they are cougars or reptilian aliens or dragons. Power thus frequently comes from connection to the land and/or the animal world; indeed, the realms of the human and animal intersect frequently, and it is the non-human beings who make the survival of the humans possible. Losing that connection to the animal and spirit worlds inevitably leads to trouble.

Celu Amberstone's fiction demonstrates clearly how authors from marginalized groups have found a rich vein of useful conventions and tropes in fantastic fiction as they seek to portray what it means to be in a subordinate social position. Her protagonists struggle with the forces that try to define them, emerging with a stronger sense of who and what they are. In a sense, they are all, like Shashil, on a spirit quest as they seek their true selves with courage and determination. Although about other worlds and other times, Amberstone's tales reflect real-world challenges and what it takes to overcome them.

Refugees

Awakening Moon, sun-turning 1

This morning I arose early and climbed to the Mother Stone on the knoll above the village. The sun was just rising above the blue mists on the lake. The path smelled of tree resin and flowering moss. I took in a deep breath, and sang to the life around me. I was shivering by the time I reached the Mother Stone and made the first of my seasonal offerings to Tallav'Wahir, our foster planet.

I cut open my arm with the ceremonial obsidian knife I carried with me, and watched my blood drip into the channel carved into the stone for that purpose. Blood. The old people say it is the carrier of ancestral memories, and our future's promise. I am a child from the stars – a refugee, driven from my true home. My blood is red, an alien color on this world. But I am lucky because this planet knows my name.

AWAKENING MOON, SUN-turning 2

I should rejoice in the renewal of life, but this Awakening Moon my heart is sad. Always before one of my daughters has been with me to share this special time. They are all gone now. My youngest daughter married last harvest and moved to a village across the lake. I miss her. My dear old man, Tree, says I should be glad to be done with that cycle of my life. But if I still crave the company of children, he is sure that my co-wife Sun Fire would be happy to share. He says this with a smile when he sees my long face, and truly the children left in the compound are more than a handful for us. But though I love them all – including my widowed sisters, it isn't quite the same. I pray that Tukta's marriage will be a happy one, and blessed with healthy children. Oh Mother, how we need healthy children.

AWAKENING MOON, SUN-turning 7

Today our Benefactors confirmed our worst fears. Earth is now a fiery cloud of poisons, a blackened cinder. When it happened, our ancient soul-link with Earth Mother enabled us to sense the disaster even from this far world across the void. Tallav'Wahir felt it too. But we told our foster planet mother that our life patterns were sound. Our Benefactors would help us. Such a tragedy would never happen here. There was a great outpouring of blood and grief at the Mother Stones all over the world. The land ceased to tremble by the time the ceremonies ended.

LEAF-BUDDING MOON, sun-turning 3

The star shuttle arrives with our new wards tomorrow – twenty-one of them for our village. What an honor to be given so many. Dra'hada says that the crew won't awaken them from cold-sleep until just prior to their arrival. When they are led out, they will be disorientated, and we will have to be patient with them. Dra'hada has assured me that our implants and theirs have been attuned to the same frequency so that we can communicate easily, and that is a relief. I wonder what these new people will be like. I am excited, and maybe a little afraid too. All the wars and urban violence we've heard about, I hope they can adjust to our simple ways. It's been a long time since our Benefactors have brought settlers to Tallav'Wahir to join us. We desperately need these newcomers. Tallav'Wahir is kind, but there is something in this adoptive environment that is hard on us too. We aren't a perfect match for our new home, but our Benefactors have great hopes for us.

LEAF-BUDDING MOON, sun-turning 4

It is moonrise, and it's been an exhausting day for all of us. I was near the front of the crowd when the shuttle set down on the landing pad. I thought I was prepared for anything. How wrong I was. They are so alien. It is hard to believe we are the same species. The situation on Earth deteriorated so fast that the ship was forced to gather what survivors were available without delay. There was no time to select the suitable. The sorting will have to be done here I suppose, and that is unfortunate. Culling is very stressful for everyone. Most of the people assigned to our village were dazed and confused, but some were angry too. Maybe they were afraid of our Benefactors, and that might account for their rude behavior. Filthy lizards indeed. They are an unsettling addition to our village, and the land feels it too.

LEAF-BUDDING MOON, sun-turning 5

Dra'hada says, even though they look and act so differently, they all come from a large city called Vancouver. We have three staying in our family's compound. When I first saw the young woman given to us, my heart pounded like a drum. I'd caught only a glimpse of her in profile, and I thought my daughter Tukta had returned to me. Then she turned to face me and the resemblance vanished. It was an unsettling experience nonetheless. Her features at times still remind me of Tukta's, but in no other way are they the same!

This girl is of medium height, golden-skinned, and very, very thin. She was wearing tight black pants, and black boots with high heels that make her walk funny. She also had on a black shirt, very sheer – I could see her tiny nipples pressed against the fabric. Over that she wore a black leather jacket with lots of silver chains. Her hair is short, spiky and blue. She has a ring in her nose and several in her ears, and a pudgy baby that cries a lot. She told us her name was Sleek. Jimtalbot, one of our other charges, says that isn't her real name, just a "street name." I'm not sure what he meant by that, but I'll wait and ask him later.

Jimtalbot is one of the few older adults left in our care. Unlike Sleek, he has pale skin, and gray streaks in his short brown hair. His face is a bit puffy, and his belly soft. Dra'hada says we will have to watch him because his heart is weak. Jimtalbot told me that he was a professor at the University of British Columbia. He has lively blue eyes and is very curious about everything. I like him the best of the lot.

Our third fosterling, given into Tree's care mostly, is a sullen, brown-skinned youth whose "street name" is Twace. He wares a bright-colored cloth tied around his head, and baggy striped pants. I don't like his angry eyes, and the color of his aura. It is filled with red and murky gray patches. When he looked around our compound, and saw the neat round dwellings with their sturdy mud walls and mossy roofs, the thatched stable for our woolly beasts, and the shady arbor where my loom sits, his mouth curled in contempt.

They are abed now – finally. Tomorrow we will have to get them suitable clothing and bring them to the Mother Stone on the knoll. I hope they won't be too frightened by the adoption ceremony.

LEAF-BUDDING MOON, sun-turning 6

We tried to prepare our fosterlings for the proceedings, but no amount of assurance on our part seemed to ease their minds. All were anxious, and some had to be dragged screaming and cursing to the Mother Stone while an elder made the cut for the required blood offering. Sleek was one of the worst. She kicked and clawed at the men who brought her forward, and no amount of assurance on my part could calm her.

When we returned home, Sleek was a mess. Her arms and face were bloody, and her alien clothes were ruined. I saw my neighbors' pitying glances as we took her away. My widowed sister and my co-wife, Sun Fire, helped me strip off her clothing and get her cleaned up. I was so ashamed for our family.

"Ignorant savages, cannibals, leave me alone, god damn you!" she shouted at us as we washed her.

"It's all right daughter, calm down. Come now, it was only a little blood; it didn't really hurt to make the gift. No one is going to eat you. The blood was given to the Stone so that our foster planet mother could taste you. Now She will know you as one of her own. We all make such offerings; it is one of the ways our Benefactors have taught us to commune with the soul of the land. Such traditions were practiced on Earth once – didn't you know that?"

"Screw traditions – and the lizards," she snarled and threw the new dress I was trying to hand her on the floor. "I want my own clothes – what have you done with my things, bitch?"

"Don't talk to your foster mother like that," my sister said. "Show her more respect."

Sleek opened her mouth to reply, but I hurried on to forestall another outburst. "I'm sorry, Sleek, but it was necessary to get rid of those alien things. They aren't in harmony with life here. You must wear and use the natural things provided by *this* planet now. Their power will help you commune with Tallav'Wahir. These ways may seem harsh to you at first, but they are important. Our elders and our Benefactors know what is best for us – truly they do."

Sleek gave me a withering look, but took the simple dress I handed her. While the fabric was over her head I heard her mumble something about ignorant savages talking to dirt. "Our Benefactors know best," she mimicked as her head cleared the opening. "Well, they're not *my* benefactors. You people are pathetic. Damned lizards have you humans living like primitive savages while they fly around in their spaceships."

Her words were meant to cut, but I thought I saw tears in the corners of her eyes so I bit back my angry response. "We know about the high technologies," I told her quietly. "We use what you would call computers, air cars and other technical things too. But to help you make the re-patterning, we decided that a simple lifestyle would be best for all of us for a time. There is no shame in living close to the land in a simple way, daughter.

"Our Benefactors teach us that technology must never interfere with our Communion with the Mother, lest we forget the Covenant, grow too greedy and destroy our new home."

Sleek's face flushed a deep crimson, and she probably would have said more rude things to me, but at that point her baby began crying in the yard outside, and she took that as an excuse to leave us. When she was gone my sister, Sun Fire and I looked at one another in exasperation. Her behavior could try the patience of a stone.

FLOWERING MOON, SUN-turning 7

The planting is over. It was a nice change to play with the children on the beach today. The water in the lake is already warm enough for a swim. Sleek and I played with them for hours in the shallows by the shore. Her face relaxed; she looked younger and seemed so happy, and that made me happy too. Maybe she and the others can adjust to our ways after all.

FLOWERING MOON, SUN-turning 9

Jimtalbot rubs his fourth finger when he thinks no one is looking. Like the others he was forced to give up everything from his past, including the thin gold ring that used to be on that finger. Just now when I went out to relieve myself, I heard someone sobbing quietly in the shadows under the te'an tree. When I went to investigate I saw Jimtalbot. I sat down beside him and took his hand. "What's so wrong?" I asked him. He sniffed and tried to pull his hand out of mine, but I held on and repeated my question.

"Nothing really – I'll be all right... I was just thinking about home – and my dead wife. She was visiting her mother in Toronto when it happened. The whole eastern part of the country was annihilated from what Dra'hada told me."

"Such thoughts are more than nothing, Jimtalbot. I can't imagine losing so much; it must be terrible. I think you and the others are very brave."

He shook his head; I could see the gleam of unshed tears in his eyes by the lantern light. "Not brave at all. Your *Benefactors* gave us no choice."

There was such harshness to his voice when he said those words that I shivered and wrapped my shawl tighter around my shoulders. "They are your Benefactors too," I pointed out to him. "Would you rather have had them leave you to die?"

He was silent for a long time; finally he said, "I don't know, Qwalshina. It is all so different here – I don't know if I have the courage to live in this place."

Surprised by his confession, I raised his hand to my lips and kissed it. "Surely you can; we are all here to love and help you. You aren't alone here – And if you wish a new wife –"

At that point he disentangled his hand from mine and stood up. "Thank you for your concern, Qwalshina. You are very kind. I think I shall go back to my bed now. Good night."

I went back to my own bed with a troubled heart. The little ring was such a small memento. Did we do right to make them give up everything? Our Benefactors advised it, but...

FLOWERING MOON, SUN-turning 25

Last night there was an argument down by the beach that ended with Sand Walker and one of the new men being injured. Everyone is so upset today, and Dra'hada was furious when he heard about it. He told me that such violence wouldn't be tolerated. Why can't the new ones see how lucky they are? These people were saved from death; why are they so angry? I don't understand them. I wish they'd never been brought here.

No, that isn't true; we need them...

KORN GROWING MOON, sun-turning 11

I had to make a difficult decision yesterday about Sleek. Her baby was suffering. She would shout and curse the babe more often than she would feed or care for the boy. Today the women's council came to take the baby away. She cursed us in the vilest terms. Judging by her behavior later, however, I think she is secretly relieved to be rid of the child. The council gave the little one to Aunty Shell to foster. Granny Night Wind says the boy is doing better already.

I look at Sleek's hard eyes and I wonder what is wrong with her. Can't she feel any emotion but anger? How could she be so indifferent to her own child's welfare? I remember how it was when we lost my oldest daughter's first born. Poor unfortunate mite – we were all distraught when he had to be culled.

KORN GROWING MOON, sun-turning 16

Our medicine woman, Granny Night Wind, thinks we will have a good crop this harvest season. Tallav'Wahir, we live in harmony with Her cycles. She feeds us, Her spirit helpers protect us, and in return we bury our shit and our dead in her rich gray soil so that She can absorb our essence, swallow our memories, and enfold us in the oneness of Her living soul. My daughter Tukta's face comes into my mind. She is so young, and so happy. Will the land love and bless her, make her one of Her favored ones? Oh, I pray it will be so.

BERRY MOON, SUN-TURNING 2

There was a great bonfire down on the beach last night. We baked fish on sticks, and ate berries cooked with sweet dumplings, till our bellies grew hard and round. In the long green twilight, we played running games. Then, someone brought out a drum and that started everyone singing and dancing. Our Twace and two boys in my cousin Rain's compound can drum very well. I danced till I thought I would fall over from exhaustion. Later Tree, Sun Fire and I crept off to a quiet place by the spring where we made sweet love under the stars. Some time during the night Tree's unmarried brother, Sand Walker, joined us and that was good too.

BERRY MOON, SUN-TURNING 9

When I was working at my loom this evening, Sleek came over unexpectedly and sat down beside me. She seemed curious, and maybe a little interested. None of my other children have the talent to be a master weaver. It would be a shame for the family to lose such a skill when I become too old for the craft. Some of our Benefactors pay high prices for our art back on their Homeworld. I let her watch for a time then I asked, "Would you like me to show you how to do this?" She shrugged, but didn't get up and leave. *Best not frighten her away*, I thought, so I just continued on with my work.

After a while she volunteered, "My grandmother used to weave – it looked something like that."

Startled, I stopped my work and turned to face her. "Really? That's very interesting. What kind of things did she make?"

"I don't remember exactly; I was pretty young when she died... I remember one thing she made though. It had bright colors; I used to tangle my fingers in its long fringes." She smiled at the memory, and added, "It was probably something ceremonial, a dance cape maybe. A lot of the old women in our band used to make them for the potlatch ceremonies."

"Pot-a-latch," My tongue stumbled over the unfamiliar word. "Was this ceremony of your people held to honor the Earth Mother?"

"I don't know; my mom never took me to one."

I went back to my weaving at that point. I could see she was becoming nervous by my questioning. *Be careful, Qwalshina, or you will frighten her away,*

I told myself. But inwardly I smiled as I twined the yarn back and forth between the rope strands on the loom. Truly our Benefactors are wise. Dra'hada knew how much I was missing Tukta, and gave me a new daughter of the same racial stock as my own. At that moment I felt very good about knowing that. It made me feel a little closer to her.

On impulse I asked her, "How old are you?"

She seemed startled by my question, and her eyes narrowed with suspicion at first then she relaxed. "The lizards didn't tell you?"

"No. I never asked our Benefactors. Is your age a secret? Would you tell me?"

She gave me another shrug. "No secret. Eighteen. Why?"

"I was just curious. Eighteen." I forced myself to go back to my weaving. *Gently, gently, Qwalshina,* I told myself. "You are about the age of my third daughter. She got married recently and moved to another village. I miss her. I'm glad you are here to take her place."

Sleek snorted. "I don't have much use for *mothers* so don't get your hopes up about making me your new daughter – or teaching me that silly string stuff either."

She made me angry then, and I allowed my evil tongue to say something cutting in return. "Maybe if you had been more willing to be *mothered* you could have done a better job of being a mother yourself, instead of abusing your baby."

Sleek jerked back as if I'd slapped her – which in a way I had. I saw the hurt in her eyes, for just a moment, and then it was gone, replaced by her habitual sullen anger. She stood up, and glared down at me with such contempt that it made my bones shiver. "You people make me sick," she spat back.

"You think you're so wonderful and know what's best for everyone, don't you? Well, let me tell you about *my* mother. She was a drunk who let her boyfriends fuck me whenever they wanted; then told me it was my fault for being a slut. I never wanted to be a mother — fuck mothers — all mothers. Who needs any of you?"

I stared after her with tear-filled eyes. Why had I said that? I'm so ashamed. Now I understand a little more why she acts the way she does, but that doesn't excuse my behavior. I must go to the Mother Stone, make an offering and try to regain my internal harmony. Like a disease these people are destroying our peace. And, if I am honest with myself I must admit that Sleek and the others frighten me. Her questions and her anger make me uncomfortable. Is she right? Are we too complacent and judgmental? I have to go help Sun Fire with the children.

KORN RIPENING MOON, sun-turning 17

The whole village is in an uproar after what happened last night. Someone stole some of Granny Night Wind's uiskajac. It was fermenting in a big wooden barrel at the back of her compound. When Sand Walker went to check on the brew, he found the barrel only half full. Granny Night Wind was furious. She threatened to give the persons responsible a bad case of "the itch" when she finds them. Whoever did it is either very brave — or crazy. She is a powerful shamanka; the spirits obey her. Still, it was funny to see her stomping around, looking under everything — people leaping out of her way — or jumping to do her bidding.

RAIN-COMES-BACK MOON, sun-turning 2

These young ones, so corrupted by poor food and alien drugs, have grown up spindly, like unhappy plants shaded from the sun. The last human crop of their tormented, polluted world is a pitiful one indeed. Will their life-patterns be suitable to mingle with ours? My people need the flow of new genes or we may perish in spite of all our Benefactor's efforts. I am so afraid for my children. The birth defects and terminations are so many. I fear for my daughter Tukta. She is so young and so happy with her new man.

Ah, but Dra'hada says, not to give up hope. We will salvage what we can from this last harvest. And if that is not enough, our Benefactors will collect the seeds of other worlds and crossbreed them with ours. Our descendants may not be the same in appearance as we are, but some part of us will survive. And the land will always remember us. Our bodies will lie in the cool ground, until the blood memories of our species have passed into the crystals of the bedrock itself.

RAIN-COMES-BACK MOON, sun-turning 4

Jimtalbot and Bethbrant were troubled by a crazy rumor they'd heard, and came this evening to ask me if it might be true.

"One of the guys from Earth, living at Black Rock Village said that Earth isn't really destroyed," Jimtalbot told me.

I looked into their troubled faces and felt a shiver run down my spine. "What? Why would he say such a thing? Of course the Earth Mother is gone. Why else would our Benefactors have brought you here?"

"Why indeed, Qwalshina?" Jimtalbot said. "Could the – uh – Benefactors be planning some weird experiment? Something that they need live humans, or human body parts for?"

I was shocked, speechless. "Experiment? No, of course not. That's preposterous. Who said such a thing? I must tell Dra'hada; who is it?"

Their expressions became closed at that point. Jimtalbot mumbled that he didn't know the man's name, but I was sure he was lying to me. He looked at Bethbrant and they started to walk away, but I stopped them. "Please wait. If you don't wish me to tell Dra'hada, Jimtalbot, I won't, but listen to me. There is no truth to this rumor. I felt Earth Mother's death agony myself – through the Communion – we all did. The pain was almost unbearable. Truly She is gone. And, there is no planned experiment. Our Benefactors only wish us well."

"If your people were also a part of their design, you might not be aware of the experiment either," Bethbrant said.

"No, we would know if they were using us in that way. We have been here for generations. My father was a man of the Tsa'La'Gui people. His ancestors were brought here when pale-skinned invaders from across a big ocean came and took their land. My mother's people came here long before my fathers. They were Crunich and lived on the island of Erin before the black-robed ones with their dead god came, and stole the island's soul. There are others from Earth Mother here too, rescued from disaster as you were. Our Benefactors wish only good for us. And, no matter our origin on Earth, we are all one people now, the children of Tallav'Wahir. There has never been any experiment. Please believe me."

When I finished talking to them, they seemed convinced that it was all a crazy, made up lie. But later the children told me that a group of our charges walked down the beach together to talk over something in private. Did I do right to promise not to tell Dra'hada? This is very troubling. I must go to the Mother Stone and tell Her my concerns.

FALLING LEAVES MOON, sun-turning 5

Sleek's tattooed friend and six other youths have developed a terrible case of "the itch." No common healing remedy has worked. Poor lads – I know they're miserable – and I shouldn't laugh at their misfortunes, but it *is* funny to watch them trying to scratch all those hard-to-reach places. Rain's twins were in on the scheme. One of them finally broke down and confessed. About half of the stolen uiskajac was brought back. Granny is keeping the offenders in suspense for one more night; but she told me privately that she would forgive them, and give them a healing salve tomorrow.

FALLING LEAVES MOON, sun-turning 25

Sleek and I took the children for a walk on the knoll today. We piled up great mountains of leaves and had fun jumping into them. I tired before they did, but felt so good just watching them. My new daughter I think loves playing like a child when none of her Earth friends are around to ridicule her. She is recreating the happy childhood she didn't have on Earth, and it is a joy to see her so.

Later we roasted siba fruit that we gathered, on sticks over an open fire, and everyone sang songs. I found myself wishing Tukta could have been there to share the day with us. When we were heading home the children raced ahead, as usual, but Sleek waited for me on the trail, and fell into step beside me as I passed. I smiled and she returned the gesture.

In the dappled light under the trees her face suddenly seemed to metamorphose into that of an ancient. Expressing wisdom far beyond her years, she said to me, "I had fun with you today, but I'm not Tukta, Qwalshina. Please try to remember that." There was no anger in her voice for once, the smells of tree resin, spicy siba, and a lazy afternoon had drained her of hostility.

Startled I paused in the trail and faced her. "I know... I had fun today too, and I'm glad you are, who you are. I wouldn't want it any other way."

"Mm... Then stop calling me Tukta."

"I don't," I protested.

She gave me a reproachful look, her eyes luminous and sad. "You're not even aware that you're doing it are you?"

Was I? Oh Mother, was I confusing her with my daughter in the physical world as well as my mind? "I'm sorry, Sleek, I *didn't* realize I'd been doing that. Do I do it often?"

She made a noncommittal sound, which I took to be acceptance of my apology. "Not often, but sometimes – like today – you forget." She shrugged, looked away, and brushed her hand across a feathery tree branch. We'd chopped off the dyed blue parts of her hair some time back, and now soft brown waves hung down past her shoulders. Up ahead one of the children called to her at that point, and she raced down the trail to catch up with the others.

I kept walking at a slower pace, thinking. I hadn't realized I'd been doing that. Her gentle rebuke caused me to question my own insecurities. It wasn't fair to Sleek if I was indeed trying to mold her into another's image for my own comfort. Why did I continue to cling to the past? Why couldn't I go on with my life – what was I afraid of? I will have to guard my tongue and my thoughts more carefully in future. I must go see Granny Night Wind; maybe she can guide me through this difficult time.

FROST MOON, SUN-TURNING 15

It's getting very cold at night now. We arrived back in the village by the lake yesterday afternoon, our pack beasts heavy-laden from the annual hunt. Soon we will hold the last harvest feast. Everyone is excited. After the festivities we will pack up everything important and leave this exposed, stormy beach. When the blue snows pile up outside, we will be safe in our warm underground lodges up the sheltered valley in the hills.

FROST MOON, SUN-TURNING 28

I walked to the Mother Stone today to say farewell till our return in Awakening Moon. The seasons have turned and the dark time is upon us once again. In the shadows along the path specters of other races that once lived here too materialized, and watched me with solemn red eyes. Their voices whispered to me on the cool wind, but I couldn't understand their alien speech. What happened to those born to this world? Our Benefactors don't know. ...

Along with my blood I poured out to the Mother my hopes and fears for the future. I hope She heard and will bless us. We are all that is left of humanity now. Can we survive? Or will this land one day absorb us back into itself as she has others who have walked these hills? Such thoughts deepened the chill in my bones, and I hurried back to the warmth of my family's compound. I want us all to live, and be happy.

The last harvest feast is tonight after the communal prayers. I'm resolved to set aside my dark mood and be happy. My pregnant daughter and others, from across the lake, are coming for the festivities. Oh, it will be good to see her. I mustn't waste any more time Sun Fire needs help with the baking.

COLD MOON, SUN-TURNING 1

I am a little achy this morning – too much good food, dancing – and definitely too much uiskajac. What a wonderful party. I danced till I thought my feet would fall off. It was too cold for lovemaking under the stars but the sweet pleasure under our warm blankets was just as good. I want to laze around in bed today, but the village will begin the packing for our move. And I have to say farewell to our departing guests. My daughter looks radiant – she is due in the Awakening Moon. What a good omen. I will miss her though. I wish I could be with her during this time. I hope she waits to have the child till I can come to her.

Sleek has disappeared again – just when I need her the most ...

COLD MOON, SUN-TURNING 12

During the good weather we were able to distract our charges with work and games played down on the beach in the evenings. Now that the blue snows are here some of them have started whining about computer games and videos again. I talked to Tomcowan today about a theatre project. Maybe that will help keep them amused.

COLD MOON, SUN-TURNING 14

As a compromise, Dra'hada is willing to send for some of the high tech equipment now in storage. If our new charges agree to study in our school, they will be allowed limited time on the equipment for entertainment pursuits. Twace and the others are dubious about the schooling part, but Dra'hada was firm with them. The Long Sleep Moons are a strain on everyone; I hope the play practices and Dra'hada's machines will help it pass in tranquility.

ICE MOON, SUN-TURNING 2

We are teaching those who wish to learn, the discipline of "The Communion." In the long nights when the snows are heavy on the land above, we journey underground, to the warm cave of the Mother. There we lie together on the floor of a large chamber, our limbs touching, and we slide into the sweet reverie that is the Deep Communion with Tallav'Wahir. We leave our bodies in the warm darkness and allow our spirits to swim upon the Great Starry River. We journey to other worlds and visit with friends light years away. None of our charges can travel so far, but for those who are willing to try, we have hope that someday they will master the technique well enough to join us.

ICE MOON, SUN-TURNING 7

Tomcowan's play was a success. It was written and performed by our charges. And I am so proud; my new daughter is such a good actress. She seemed to shine like a jewel when we offered her our praise. Our fosterlings told us the story of their lives in the lost city of Vancouver. Parts were funny, and some things were sad. Much of it I didn't understand, but in spite of that, the performance was very moving. The elders will tell stories of our own history tonight. I hope our fosterlings will like them. There is so much for us to share and weave together if we are to become one people.

ICE MOON, SUN-TURNING 15

In the aftermath of Tomcowan's play an air of desolation has settled over our charges. It is very disheartening. The long gloomy days indoors have given the memories of their lost home an unexpected poignancy. More fights today.

Just now I found Jimtalbot staring moodily into the flames of our fire. I sat beside him and asked why he and the others were still grieving for such a horrible place.

He looked at me with his sorrowful blue eyes and said, "It wasn't all bad there, Qwalshina. My wife and I lived comfortably in a nice house by the ocean. Along with the bad, was a lot of good too. Art, music, fine literature, advances in science and medicine, we had a lot to be proud of. As hard as it was for people like Sleek and Twace back home I think they miss it as much as I do."

"Yes, I'm sure they do, and I can't understand that either."

He shrugged. "Home is home, no matter how bad it is, and you can't help caring when it's gone – if it's gone."

If it's gone? I didn't want to get bogged down in that conversation again, so I began a new topic. "Caring? Why didn't the people of your city care enough to protect suffering children who starved on your city streets? Why didn't they care enough to honor the Earth Mother and not destroy what were her gifts to you? Can you honestly say that life here has been so terrible that you would wish to go back?"

He was silent for a long time, just staring into the flames. Finally he tossed another stick onto the fire and shook his head. "I don't know, Qwalshina."

"Don't know?" I was confused and upset myself by then so I left him. Vancouver sounded like such a terrible place. How could they possibly miss it and want to return.

ICE MOON, SUN-TURNING 19

The rumors about Earth have surfaced again, and this time I'm sure Dra'hada has heard them. Perhaps the play wasn't such a good idea after all. Everyone is getting tired of the cold and the confinement. The books have been read and reread, lessons and amusements are boring, and food and drink grow stale. Tempers are short. I try to sleep as much as I can. For us, this time is a natural phenomenon to be endured. For our charges, it is a torment beyond belief. Our warm dark homes anger or depress them. The snow is too deep, not the right color, too cold – the litany is endless. I'm going back to my bed.

SUN-COMES-BACK MOON, sun-turning 7

When I lie upon my communion mat and close my eyes I can feel the deep stirring in the land, and my body responds to it gladly. The sap is rising, and the snow melting, and my daughter tells me her belly is nearly bursting. The sun is warm on my back when I collect the overflowing buckets of sap from the trees in the sugar bush. And, wonder of wonders, our Sun Fire is pregnant again. Tree is taking a lot of teasing for starting a new family at his age; but we are so pleased. This time the baby — all the babies will be healthy — I just know it.

SUN-COMES-BACK MOON, sun-turning 28

One of the great ships from the Homeworld is coming. Dra'hada is ecstatic. Poor creature – this past year-turning has been so hard on him. What with all the villagers' and fosterlings' complaints to sort out and the unease of the Mother's Spirit Guardians to placate, it is no wonder that our Benefactor has aged visibly. It will do all of us good to have Benefactors from the Homeworld here for the renewal ceremonies. Perhaps they will be able to put those rumors about Earth's survival to rest once and for all.

The ship will be here by the time the snow is gone, so Dra'hada tells me. I wonder if they will bring a new mate for our dear teacher? It will be a great celebration; other villages are coming to join us. Everyone is excited, even our young fosterlings.

AWAKENING MOON, SUN-turning 4

We are back in our village by the lake again. Our compound survived the storm season without needing many repairs. That is good because the ship will be here soon and there is so much to do before our guests arrive.

During all the confusion Sleek went missing again. When she crept back into the compound just before the evening meal I was so angry I shouted at her. She of course shouted right back. Why, oh why, does she continue to be so irresponsible! I'm trying not to compare her to Tukta, but it is so hard.

AWAKENING MOON, SUN-turning 10

My heart is on the ground. The village is overflowing with guests. I'm trying very hard not to let my personal tragedy spoil the festive mood for others. My daughter's baby was born deformed and was – oh I can't even write down the words... The tragedy happened the night before last; her husband's aunt told me when she arrived today. Tears blur my vision as I try to write this. Oh Mother how could this happen – again.

Oh, Tukta, my dear sweet Tukta! I want desperately to go to her, take her in my arms and kiss away the pain. But I can't, not until after the ceremonies are over. What am I thinking of? She isn't a child anymore. I can't make this terrible hurt go away by my presence. And I have obligations to the People that take precedence over personal concerns. I must stay; I must be here to greet our Benefactors when the ship comes tomorrow. The Renewal Ceremony at the Mother Stone this year will be very important.

AWAKENING MOON, SUN-turning 11

When I looked into the faces of our guests from the Homeworld today, I felt such a rage building up inside me that I could hardly breathe at times. Granny Night Wind sensed my disharmony, and made me drink a potion to settle my spirit. This new emotion I feel frightens me. What if we are living a lie – what if the people from Earth are right? I hate them! Why did they have to come here? Maybe they should have been left to die on their god-cursed world!

AWAKENING MOON, SUN-turning 12

Our compound is quiet tonight; we took in no guests for the feasting. I can hear the sounds of merriment going on around us as I write this. The little ones don't understand. Sun Fire has taken them to the fire down on the beach. I am glad. My old man Tree is resting in the bedroom behind me. His nearness right now is a comfort.

To my surprise Sleek hasn't joined the revelers. She was standing in the doorway when I looked up from my pad. I wanted to say something encouraging to her, but I feel too dead inside to make the effort.

She watched me for a long moment in silence then said, "I-I'm sorry about your daughter, Qwalshina. Sun Fire said something went wrong and the baby's dead. Is that true – or did the damned lizards kill it?"

Her unspoken thought seemed to ring in my mind, *Filthy lizards, I told you they couldn't be trusted.* Suddenly I felt my anger leap up like oil poured onto flames. I hated her at that moment with all my heart, and maybe she felt it, because she staggered backward, and grabbed the doorpost for support. Why was she here – and healthy? Why had she, an unfit mother, had a healthy baby, when my dear sweet Tukta could not? Tukta loves her new husband, I thought, and now our Benefactors will probably want her to choose a new mate – it is unfair.

When I made no answer, and only glared at her, Sleek's expression crumpled, and she disappeared back into the night.

After she was gone Tree came out of the bedroom. He didn't reproach me for my cruelty; he only took me in his arms and led me to our bed. I lay down beside him, buried my face in the warmth of his chest and cried.

When I could control myself enough to speak, I said, "I'm so ashamed. The one time she tried to comfort someone else, I was unkind to her. Like a mean-spirited hag I pushed her away. Why was I so cruel to her, Tree? I don't understand her or myself anymore."

"Hush now, my flower," Tree soothed. "You are tired, and grieving. People say and do things at such a time that they don't truly mean. I know you care about her, and she does too. I will speak to her tomorrow. Go to sleep, my heart, all will be well."

I drifted into sleep, as he suggested, but deep in my heart I knew all would not be well – not for a long time – and maybe not ever again.

AWAKENING MOON, SUN-turning 13

The most terrible thing has happened. Oh, it is so terrible I can hardly think of it without bursting into tears all over again. Sleek is dead, and so are ten others, one of them a native man from Cold Spring village. Tallav'Wahir, forgive me. I saw her sneaking out of our compound, and I did nothing to stop her. Did I drive her into joining those foolish people with my hard looks and resentment? Was I just another mother who failed her?

It was late in the afternoon when it happened. Most of our visiting Benefactors and other guests had taken air cars down the lake to visit Black Rock Village. I was just helping Sun Fire settle the children for their naps when a loud rumbling whine brought me, and most of the adults still home in the village racing to the shore. The great ship resting on the sand was making terrible noises, and trembling violently by the time we arrived. From within its opened hatchway we heard screaming – human screaming.

We looked at one another; our eyes round as soup bowls. Then, all the noise and trembling stopped as abruptly as it started. We waited, but nothing further happened. Finally Granny Night Wind and I walked to the stairway and called out to the crew left on duty inside. At first no one answered, but when the old woman started up the stairs, a weak voice from within warned her to come no closer. We exchanged glances, and then I said to the people in the ship, "Honored Benefactors, is something wrong? Can we help you?"

"No, you can't help. Come no closer — it may kill you too if you try to enter."

Kill us? I was taller than granny; I peered into the dimness of the open hatch. My nose caught the metallic scent of blood, before I saw it. There on the floor, blood – red blood. The benefactor's blood is brown. I shivered, a claw of fear tearing at my heart. What had happened in there? Oh, Mother, where was Sleek? I turned back to Granny. Had she seen the blood on the floor too? I stepped down off the stair, my mind in shock. People called to me, but I couldn't answer. I heard the sound of the air cars returning, and then people running past me. I swayed and would have fallen, but suddenly Tree's arms were around me, hugging me to his chest.

"Qwalshina, what's happened?"

He was warm and solid, smelling of budding leaves and smoky leather. Against his chest, I shook my head. No words could get past the aching lump in my throat.

The visiting Benefactors rushed into their ship, and soon after Dra'hada appeared and told us to return to our homes. He wouldn't answer the shouted questions put to him. "Everything is in order now. No need to fear. Go back to your homes. Tonight at the Big Sing I will tell you all that has happened."

Granny Nigh Wind added her own urging to the gathered people and soon most drifted away. I stayed; I refused to let Tree and Sun Fire lead me away. When Dra'hada came over to us, I clutched his scaly hand and begged, "Please, honored teacher, tell me what has happened."

Dra'hada's headcrest drooped, and he patted my hand. "Go home, Qwalshina. You can't do anything to help here. Go home with your family."

"Damn you, I'm not a child. Tell me what's happened. Is Sleek in there?" I heard Tree and Sun Fire's gasps of surprise at my disrespect, but I was too frightened to care. I had to know.

For just a moment Dra'hada's headcrest flattened and I saw the gleam of long teeth under his parted black lips. I shuddered, but stood my ground. I had to know. Then he let go his own anger, and looked at me solemnly. "I never assumed you were a child, Qwalshina; I am sorry if you think that. All right, I will tell you. Yes, Sleek is in there – dead."

I continued to stare at him, willing him to finish it. He sighed and finally continued, "It seems that the rumor about Earth still existing took root stronger in other villages than it did here. All during the harsh weather this cancer has been growing among the new refugees. A man named Carljameson wanted to take our ship and go back to Earth. There were others who helped him try. What they didn't know, or couldn't understand, is that the great ships from the Homeworld are sentient beings. They aren't shells of dead metal like the machines of Earth. When our crew was threatened, the ship itself responded by killing the intruders in a most painful way."

Dra'hada refused to tell me the details. He could sense how upset I was, and told Tree to take me home. Later I learned Carljameson and his war band forced their way on board the ship with the help of the man from Cold Spring. They stole weapons from somewhere and injured one of our Benefactors during the struggle. With so many new people here, and everybody celebrating, no one took note of the conspirators' odd behavior.

Ah, why didn't I go after Sleek when I saw her leave? I was selfish and careless. I was grieving for my daughter, and I was so tired of fighting with her. I blame myself in part for her tragic death. Could I have done more to make her a part of our family?

AWAKENING MOON, SUN-turning 14

There is a great council being held among our Benefactors aboard the ship. Communications with the Homeworld have been established. Because of the man from Cold Spring's involvement, not only the newcomers' fate, but also our own, will depend on the Council's decision.

Some of our Benefactors claim that we are a genetically flawed species. We should all be eliminated, and this world reseeded with another more stable species. Others like our dear Dra'hada counsel that that is too harsh a decision. We have lived here the required seven generations and more. We are not to blame for the assault. They counsel that those of us, who have bred true to the Ancient Way, should be allowed to continue on, either as we are, or interbred with another compatible species to improve our bloodlines.

They are meeting on the ship now.

Around me the land continues to sing its ancient song of renewal. The Mother will not intercede for us with our Benefactors. She is wise, but in the passionless way of ancient stone. In the darkness last night the people met in the village square to sing the Awakening songs, as we have always done. Tears in my eyes, I lifted up my voice with the rest. I was afraid – we all were. Just before dawn I climbed to the Mother Stone.

WHAT WILL THE DAY BRING to my people, Life or termination? I lean my head against the stone's solid bulk and breathe in the smells of new growth and the thawing mud in the lake. Blood. The old people say it is the carrier of ancestral memory and our future's promise. The stone is cold. I'm shivering as I open a wound on my forearm and make my offering. My blood is red, an alien color on this world...

An Act of Power

On the highway a logging truck roared by, cascading gravel over the drainage ditch's lip. Candace flinched as a piece of debris stung her cheek. Tears threatened, but she ignored them, continuing her frantic search for the lost medicine bundle. Cougar claws, bits of crystal and other sacred objects tucked into a rawhide bag, then wrapped in a piece of red trade-cloth, how could it hide among the grey thistles and dry grass of summer? Her trembling hands parted another clump of tall weeds...

Oh, Creator, was that rusty-red patch blood – her blood?

Again the swoosh, swoosh of cars overhead. Suddenly dizzy, Candace dropped to her knees. Sobbing, she covered a pale oval face with her hands, her brown hair tumbling about her shoulders.

"Oh, Grandma! What were you doing out here so late last night? Why did you secretly leave the logging protest – to walk home alone?"

The news of the old woman's death had swept through the Singing Wind Reservation like wildfire, fueling the growing rage against the outsiders logging the watershed on tribal land. Grandma Dorothy had been a respected elder. But like many others, both White and Native, living along these narrow mountain roads, she'd been struck down by a speeding wood-chip truck. Flung into the ditch she'd been left to die – like a deer – just another piece of road kill. The unexpected tragedy had left Candace feeling heart-sick and abandoned – just like when the social worker took her away.

Then through her tears she heard a bird singing of joy and hope among the aspens on the far slope. She took a shuddering breath, got to her feet and with a grim determination renewed her search.

At the sound of tumbling gravel she whirled and saw a tall figure in dusty jeans and a black T shirt sliding down the embankment. Catching his balance at the bottom, he smiled and headed in her direction. A ball cap and long black braids framed the newcomer's high-cheekboned, caramel-skinned face. Recognizing Jonas she relaxed. Did he care that much? Had he gotten worried?

Long before granddaughter Candace had shown up, looking for "her roots" Grandma Dorothy had been Jonas's teacher. Jonas was a good man, fighting to protect the People's land. She was unbelievably lucky to have such a respected young man for her friend and lover.

Jonas threw an arm about her shoulder and kissed her. "You scared the shit out of everyone at the community hall, Candi, running off like that –"

Another truck roared by, drowning out the rest of his words. Candace shook her head, resisting his attempts to steer her up the slope. "Jonas, why did she sneak into the medicine lodge at the camp and take away our family's sacred bundle?"

"I don't know."

"What was she afraid of?"

He laughed, dismissing the idea. "Afraid? She had Cougar's medicine to protect her. She wasn't afraid of anything. Come on. Lets go."

She stepped back and glared. "No! I have to find Grandma's medicine bundle first – keep it safe."

"It's not here, Candi. Jimmy already looked."

"Jimmy? What does your cousin have to do with this?"

Voice remaining calm, he said, "Jimmy picked up the two kids who found the body." He waved his hand, the gesture encompassing the trash and weeds choking the narrow ravine. "After he dropped them off at the police station in town he came back."

Though she didn't care for the man, Jimmy *was* a "traditional." Better him than the cops. "Did he find it?

Jonas shook his head and guided her towards the waiting car. "No. He looked around while he waited for the cops to show up, but found nothing. Let's go. Maybe they took it away when they removed her body."

"But what if the cops don't have it, Jonas? If witches were to find it –"

His arm went about her waist, urging her forward. "Get serious, Candi. The Medicine will turn up – when it wants to."

A car horn honked. Firming up his grip, he urged her up the slope. "Relax. If the cops don't have the bundle, we'll ask Cougar and Grandma's spirit to help us find it when we do the ceremony."

At the top of the embankment Candace shrugged out of his grasp and stared, incredulous. "How can you even consider going ahead with that crazy ritual after what has happened?"

Expression grim, he studied her for a long moment, then finally said, "Have to. In spite of those apples on the band council getting everyone excited about more jobs, the logging has to stop."

"But –"

"No buts, Candi." His voice gentle, caressing, he held her gaze. "The land and the river will die unless we stop them. You know that."

Yes, she did know – she'd seen it in her visions...

Suddenly dizzy again, she heard a thunderous roar. The vision of dusty highway and brush-clogged ditch blurred, replaced by an iron-gray sky pouring dirty rain onto hills devoid of trees. Mudslides dammed up the river, flooding the valley, killing people and animals. ...

A hot wind gusted across her face, snarled in her hair, then whirled down the ravine, bending the brush in its passing. *The Evil One is near. Beware, Cougar's child.*

Candace reeled and would have fallen if Jonas hadn't caught her. Breath coming in ragged gasps, she desperately prayed not to be swept away by her recurring nightmare.

"The visions again?" When she nodded, he tightened his hold. "Don't be afraid, Candi. I'm going to take care of you – you're my girl, right?"

"But Grandma wasn't sure about your ceremony. She told me –"

"She wanted us to stop the loggers – no matter what, right?"

Still shaken by the force of the vision, Candace nodded and allowed him to lead her to the waiting car.

A LOW WOOD AND CONCRETE structure that had once been an Indian Affairs school, the Singing Wind's community hall was stifling. Sitting round a scarred table in the alcove off the kitchen afforded the warriors' council some privacy from the grannies knitting and gossiping over by the bleachers, and the guys bouncing a ball in the center of the floor, but the wooden partition also cut off the breeze coming through the open doors across the gym.

Candace sighed and wiped her forehead with a napkin. Would they ever stop arguing and finish, so they could get out of this heat? The protesters' camp among the big trees on Copper Creek would be cool and shady at this time of day...

The lawyer on loan from a national save the environment association ran a hand through his thinning shoulder-length hair and cleared his throat. "The Band Council's argument that logging will bring more jobs to the reservation will seem quite attractive to many of the unemployed here. You might want to reconsider your strategy. Maybe talking about spirits isn't the best way to approach an international corporation, the media, or those on the reserve who don't agree with your position."

The two elders at the end of the table who had been smoking and quietly listening chose that moment to rise and walk outside. The rest of the warriors arranged their dark faces into the mask of blankness put on for whites. The unspoken accusation of "racist bastard" rang as clear as a bell in the heavy silence.

How could the lawyer be so ignorant of First Nations protocol? She wondered. Hadn't anyone briefed him before coming here?

Through a break in the partition Candace could see the elders heading for their trucks. Several children were kicking a soccer ball around the dusty parking lot. Acutely aware of her own pale skin and shaky acceptance on the rez, she wished she was out there with the kids instead of sitting here.

Dressed in designer jeans and cowboy shirt, she supposed the lawyer was trying his best to fit in. Seeking an ally perhaps, he raised an inquiring eyebrow when he caught her eye. Candace flushed and looked away. Secretly she might agree with him, but she wasn't going to say so. The silence dragged painfully on.

In the kitchen her mom's sister, Aunti Margaret's booming laugh stood out from the murmur of women's voices. Plump with arms as strong as any man's, Margaret was her favorite relation. She could remember her vaguely from her childhood. A smiling woman, Aunti had always offered her hard candy and bannock, whenever Candace had been dumped at her house. Maybe she should go and help with the protestors' dinner.

As she made to rise, Jonas put a hand on her arm and she slumped back into her seat. His eyes danced with amusement as if divining her thoughts. He wasn't going to let her sneak away so easily.

Seeing no support, the lawyer's face turned a bright red. Jonas squeezed Candi's hand under the table, then rocked his chair back on two legs and folded his arms across his chest. A mocking smile played about his full lips as he said, "So, you think repeating the teachings of our elders is nonsense? Like maybe they are senile, eh?"

The lawyer threw up his hands. "I never said that. I'm just trying to make you understand how the other side will use what you say against you—"

Red bandanna tied about his forehead, Apache style, a guy named Johnny blurted, "It doesn't matter what we say. The Guardian will speak for us now, in this world and in the spirit world, where the logging corporation's black magicians work their spells. The logging's gonna' stop."

"I see." The lawyer glanced at Candace and rolled his eyes. Candace flushed and sipped her coffee.

Realizing she wasn't going to support him, he began piling papers into his battered briefcase. Finished, he shut it with a snap, looked Jonas in the eye and muttered, "I have to get back. Bobby Elk Hunter's arraignment is this afternoon. Think about what I said and call my office when you want to set up another meeting."

Jonas made a noncommittal gesture. "Yeah, sure, we'll do that."

The lawyer turned and walked stiff-backed from the hall.

"Stupid prick," Jimmy growled. "We don't need his kind anyway."

But they did need that white lawyer, or someone like him, Candace knew. If the protests continued more people than Bobby Elk Hunter and his brother were going to end up behind bars.

Were Jonas and the others just going to let the only lawyer willing to work for free walk out – maybe never coming back? Just because he'd made a little mistake and unwittingly insulted Joe Black Bear and the others supporting the blockade didn't mean he was a racist.

Stick by your convictions, the voice of her foster father echoed in her mind. *Now is no time to forget what we've always taught you.*

He was nearly to his car now, but if they hurried...

No, she wouldn't forget. Holding an image of her foster dad, a professor at UBC, sitting in his book-lined study as a talisman against her fears, she gripped her hands together under the table to stop them shaking, and took a deep breath. But when she finally managed to choke the words out, her voice was barely above a whisper. "Please. Stop him. Maybe that guy knows what he's talking about."

"Trust a breed to take the white man's side every time." Someone, leaning against the wall spoke loud enough for Candace to hear.

Feeling like a fool, and hating the flush that she knew was coloring her cheeks, Candace cursed the impulse that had made her speak out.

"Pull in your claws, Kitten." The look of disapproval on Jonas's face made her insides churn.

Scent of male sweat and crushed fir boughs, dark eyes smiling down at her, raven-black hair falling over them like a veil, the memory of their love-making last night blotted out all other concerns.

How could she ever bear to lose him?

"I'm sorry. I just meant – I just wanted – if someone else gets arrested, what are we going to do without a lawyer?"

Sitting to her right, her cousin Roseanne whispered, "Candi, chill out. Jonas will figure it out, so don't worry." Plump and usually cheerful, she seemed overly anxious. Had Jimmy been slapping her around again?

She patted her cousin's hand. "But I am worried, because we need him. He didn't mean to insult Grandpa Joe."

Then, as her heart gave a lurch, she took a ragged breath and added in a slightly louder voice, "I don't think Grandma Dorothy –"

"The elder was sharing her wisdom with us long before you started hanging around, so don't try to tell us what she would say," a lean man named Arty, recently back from a peace-keeping mission abroad snapped.

"Yeah, man. She loved the big trees – a true inspiration," a guy with dreads and a greasy blond beard agreed. "She looked like such a sweet old lady, but what a temper. She wouldn't take no sass from any fuckin' cop." He shook his head in admiration, a tear spilling from his eye.

A true inspiration.

Candace felt her own tears gathering and shook her head to clear it. "I know, Arty. But like the lawyer said, we need to get our demands across in a rational way to everybody – so they won't dismiss us without listening –"

Jonas looked deep into her eyes. "Is that you or your white foster parents talking, Kitten?"

Candace felt the heat colouring her cheeks. She'd done it again, spoken when she should have kept her big mouth shut!

"Who cares what they think!" Jimmy snapped. Tall, burly and loud, he slammed his cup down, spilling hot coffee.

Candace flinched. He saw her reaction and smirked. "You think we're wrong to speak of our traditions?"

"I never said that! Stop putting words in my mouth," she snapped. Jimmy's bullying ways infuriated her.

"He's not. Candi, please don't be angry," Roseanne said, twisting her hands together. "Jimmy would never do that. Would you, Honey?"

Jimmy slurped his coffee and leaned back in his chair. "'Course not, Darlin'." There was that arrogant smirk again, Candace didn't believe a word of it. Jimmy folded his meaty arms across his chest, and looked down his nose at her. "They'll learn different soon enough. When the spirits we called taste the sacrifice –"

Jimmy closed his mouth abruptly at a hand gesture from Jonas

Hot blood dripping onto a mossy stone, scent of heavy smoke smothering breath... Choking back a scream – Candace felt the blood leave her face and willed the memory away. She shook her head, ignoring the dark chanting echoing in her mind, shivering in spite of the heat. Sacrifice ...

Leave me alone, Go away, GO AWAY!

Jonas leaned over her, his manner attentive. "Kitten, are you all right?" he murmured next to her ear.

Stomach churning, Candace felt the fear and emptiness welling up inside her. Why was she trying to make Jonas and her new friends angry?

When she'd arrived at Singing Wind Reserve in late spring, final exams at university finished for the year, the mixture of hippies and local Aboriginals protesting logging of the band's watershed seemed like an answer to her prayers. But beneath the surface of reservation politics dark currents of power twisted and boiled in the Unseen World. Grandma Dorothy was dead – and there were rumors of witch wars being whispered about in the shadows.

Bad Medicine...

Witches...

Her foster dad would laugh at such a notion.

She could hear the tremor in her own voice as she said, "The ceremony was a failure. There is no new guardian. And what could a human bound to a cougar do? Even if that were possible – which it isn't. The loggers or the RCMP would just shoot a big cat if they saw it hanging round a worksite."

Johnny chuckled. "Who said they would see it?"

"They wouldn't," Jimmy agreed with a sneer. "Until it's too late."

Jonas slammed his chair back onto all four legs and rose. "Lets get back to camp. We have work to do."

WITHOUT GRANDMA DOROTHY'S shielding love, Candace became a marked woman in the days that followed the funeral. Her family's medicine bundle had vanished. She hadn't taken it – didn't know where it was – but nobody believed her!

Tonight when the cooking crew brought dinner up to camp Auntie Margaret – whom she thought loved her, had accused her in front of everyone of stealing it – said she was a witch!

And Jonas, the bastard, who claimed to be her man – and *knew* she didn't have it – just stood there, not saying a word. Auntie Margaret would probably have believed him if he'd made the slightest effort to defend her!

"You're just like your mom, no damn good!" Uncle Leonard had said, echoing her aunt's accusations.

Suddenly her foot slid sideways into a pothole on the dark logging road, and she tumbled onto her hands and knees. Behind her in the camp, she heard Jonas shout, "Candi? Where are you, Kitten? Come back. We need too talk."

Rocking back and forth with the pain, Candace lifted her face to the starry sky, her teeth bared in a silent scream. Damn, she didn't need this. Not after everything else that had gone wrong.

"Candi? Please don't go." Who was that calling now... Roseanne?

"Candi, it's dangerous. Jimmy saw cougar tracks by the creek this morning. Please come back."

Cougar tracks.

She put a hand over her mouth to stifle a hysterical laugh. Had the big cat come looking for her? No, they were just trying to scare her – well, she wasn't listening anymore. She was leaving – tonight!

You promised the Land and the Ancestors, the Wind whispered.

Stifling a sob, Candace gingerly lifted the hem of her long flowered skirt and squinted at the damage. The cuts on her hands and knees burned, like a hundred bee stings and her ankle hurt, but her injuries weren't serious. She could make it off the mountain down to the highway. In the camp drums sounded and people began singing, drowning out the pleas for her return.

It was dark under the trees, the moon barely visible through the branches. She should have brought a flashlight. She shivered. And a jacket. How could it be so cold in summer? Candace dabbed a trickle of blood with her torn skirt, and looked around for something to use as a walking stick. It would be too humiliating if she was forced to go back to camp now.

Ah, there. That branch leaning against the big fir – yes, it would do. Without her noticing, blood from one of her cuts stained a pebble in the road.

Like her foster mom had said the last time she called, she needed to get back in school. In her mind's eye her foster father's calm blue eyes weighed, judged. *The past is better forgotten. But well educated young people of vision can help bring their indigenous communities into a healthy and prosperous future, my dear. Isn't that what we've always taught you?*

"Yes, Daddy."

If she were honest she would have to admit that there had been tension between her and her mom's family ever since her return. University educated and raised among Whites, her cousins thought her stuck up. And she in turn thought the drinking and abuse on the rez both disgusting and frightening. Well, it didn't matter now. It was over between her and Jonas. She was leaving.

A knot of sadness rose up to choke her at the thought. In spite of everything that had gone wrong since grandma's funeral she felt a deep heart's bond to this land and the people of Singing Wind. The undefined feeling would always haunt her, never changing – no matter where she wandered. This land, not the big city was her true home.

Candace swallowed hard, and kept slamming the butt of her walking stick against the flinty road. "Keep moving. It's still a long way to the highway."

A rustling off to her left suddenly jerked her out of her reverie. She froze, listening. The camp wasn't in that direction.

The Cougar glides easily between the worlds. For those blessed to know its favor it is a powerful spirit guide and guardian.

Candace shivered, turning in a slow circle. Eerie phantasms seemed to creep through the shadows under the trees. As she focused her attention on them, they blurred, melting away into the gloom without a trace. Leaves rustled under the trees, sounding like quiet laughter.

When Cougar hunts, it chooses its prey among those most vulnerable. A silky voice whispered.

"Jonas? Is that you?" Limping and bloody, maybe she'd been a fool to go off by herself in cougar country? Stupid, stupid, Roseanne had tried to warn her...

Were the shadows concealing angry spirits, a flesh-and-blood cougar, or just some ignorant, drunken loggers trying to sneak up and attack the protestors' like they'd done at Little Falls Creek?

Candace lifted her stick in a threatening gesture. "Hey, who's out there?" Trembling with a mixture of fear and indignation, she stood her ground in the middle of the road, nostrils flaring like a wild animal, hoping to catch the scent.

Only silence answered her, but she was certain something was out there. She could still feel the tingling at the back of her neck.

Then the gray silhouette of a deer bounded out of the trees and rocketed across the road in front of her. Candace gasped, nearly dropping her stick in surprise. Sucking in a great lungful of air, she exhaled it with a low chuckle. Cougars and invading loggers indeed, her mind was running away with her tonight. "Sorry, four-legged brother, I didn't mean to frighten you, sorry," she called after the retreating animal.

Around a pile of gravel and large rock displaced from an old mudslide, the logging road plunged into a dark hollow. About halfway through the dip, Candace smelled burning sage, cedar and breathed in the medicine smoke.

Grandma Dorothy's ghost walked out of the underbrush and fell into step beside her. As in life, her long gray hair was tied back from her round brown face by a leather thong, and there was a black woolen shawl around her shoulders. To Candace's dismay Grandma's hands held no medicine bundle. Fearing to look the spirit in the face, she dropped her eyes.

The ghost's voice was a mournful wail upon the night wind. *I'm sorry, dear one. I've been a foolish old woman. I've taught you best I could in the time we had together. You must stop them – stop the evil.*

Candace flinched, shaking her head in denial. A low moan escaped her dry throat. "Please, Grandma, I can't stop the logging all by myself. But I'm going back to university in the fall. I'll forget about art classes; I'll study ecology instead. I'll write letters, help with fundraising, talk to people at the university and the newspapers. The loggers won't destroy this place; I swear. I'll find some way to stop them –"

Her expression pitying, the ghost shook her head. *You don't understand yet. Do you, my girl? Only courage and blood can stop the evil now. The ghost glanced behind them. You haven't much time, Granddaughter. Choose well, my dear one.* The ghost watched her solemnly for a long moment; then she faded back into the gloom.

Not much time? Fear a stinging goad, Candace stared at the empty air, then quickened her pace.

Some time later Candace saw a break in the forest ahead. With a sigh of relief She stepped out into the open. Across the valley tree covered ridges faded into black against the night sky. Behind them, on the far peaks, ragged patches of last winter's snow glowed silver in reflected moonlight. Down below, tiny houses and patchwork fields lay strung out along the river. A goat bleated a sleepy complaint, and then all was quiet again.

The Night Wind breathed strands of hair across her face. *You must help us stop the evil.*

"No. I can't stay. I'm sorry –"

Leaving? No, no you aren't going anywhere. You belong to us.

Laughter, mirthless laughter. Oh, Spirits, who was laughing at her?

Scent of blood, cloying smoke, no escape... Candace hugged herself. Her nipples felt hard, aching in the gusts of cool wind off the peeks. Cold, god she was so cold; was she suffering from the first stages of hypothermia?

Startled by a deep rumbling, she made the mistake of looking down into the valley. Massive pale hulk, merciless glowing yellow eyes, the monster was coming for *her* this time. Candace screamed, and falling to her bruised knees screamed again, green eyes wide with terror.

Then through the growing panic, she thought she heard her grandma speaking to her. *Courage, my girl, fight them. You must be strong.*

As suddenly as it had come, the vision was gone. Taking a deep breath she rubbed a hand across her eyes and stood. There was no monster – what a crazy notion! On the highway that paralleled the river she saw only another wood-chip truck speeding along. Shaking an impotent fist in its direction, she snarled, "Damn trucks. They're always in a hurry – always taking chances on these narrow, winding roads!"

Mocking laughter in her head, *Who will it kill this time, a deer, an elk – another you love?*

"Shut up, shut up. Leave me alone, damn you!"

Candace laughed, balancing on the knife's edge of hysteria. Talking to herself; she was going crazy. No, no it was only the cold – she was so cold.

THE ROAD OFF THE MOUNTAIN seemed endless. Her pace slowed to an agonized shuffle as the night wore on. She was so cold and tired. But she had to get to town – call her folks – have them wire her a bus ticket.

Through the miasma of fatigue dulling her senses, she felt a stone bounce off the side of her sandal then continue down the road in front of her. Candace froze. Warning chills ran down her spine. Nothing was visible behind her, but she could feel – something – a dark presence, gliding through the shadows. Did she smell a musky feline odor? The night masked him, yet she was certain this time that she could detect the hunter's presence.

Water in a road-side stream murmured, *Death is stalking.*

An act of power, a gift of the self to save the land, the Stars cried.

Courage, the Wind breathed.

Vengeance for the blood of the ancestors and what has been lost, the Earth whispered. *You belong to us.*

Ignoring the voices, her sandals slapped up clouds of dust in her wake. Gait uneven, her ankle shot spears of fire up her leg. Strong, she was strong – like her ancestors. She laughed, the sound brittle and ragged. Damn them all, she wasn't going to surrender to the pain, the cold or the darkness. Almost there, she could make it.

Just ahead the last pillars of old-growth trees towered over the logging road. As she passed inside, all the night sounds became muted, as if she had stepped into a natural cathedral. Grandma's ghost, and the Spirits of the Land were waiting. Candace stopped and held out her arms to them. their expectations were too much, an overwhelming burden.

The hunter padded out of the trees and crouched on the road above her. Moonlight and leaf shadow dappled his tawny hide. Golden eyes watched her with a wary attention. His nostrils widened as he caught her musky female scent. The tip of his long tail curled and uncurled as he pondered the mystery of her.

Life or death awaits you; life or death awaits this land.

Candace looked into the big cat's eyes, with their vertically slit pupils, and saw the unyielding pronouncement of her fate. The meaningless life awaiting her back in the city crystallized into one sharp moment of agony. She couldn't help her people by continuing at the university; it was a lie. If she let the loggers and the politicians destroy this beautiful valley, what reason could she find to go on living?

The air tingled with the gathering of power. She moaned softly and dropped her stick. Covering her face with her hands, she sank onto her knees, shivering uncontrollably. Addressing the spirits directly, she sobbed, "I don't want to die."

At the sound of her voice the cougar's tail increased its arc. A warning rumble began deep in his throat, but he gave no other sign of his intent.

When death comes to claim your body, is it not better to give life to another than to rot in a concrete box as the despoilers teach?

"Ye-s-s."

Is your love for this land a true Heart-Bond?

"Yes, I love this land, but –"

There is no greater gift to offer than the gift of oneself. Give us freely of your soul's power. Come to us, Warrior Woman, and be transformed.

Candace smelled burning sage and cedar again. Beyond in the dark forest the ghosts of the ancestors began singing a Medicine Song. The sound mingled with the wind passing through heavy tree branches.

A power song, calling those who wander the night to witness an act of power.

Then, a sound like thunder shattered the sacred chant. Sharp stones cut into Candace's knees; she could feel the ground tremble under her.

WAS THAT THE RUMBLE of another chip truck? Yes. Was the vehicle coming this way? Sharp-edged and bright, hope flared like a match in the darkness; then died before the candle of deliverance could be lit. The sound came no closer, disappearing once more into the gloom.

"What are you waiting for?" Candace snarled at the cat. "Do it, before I lose my nerve and spoil everything!"

He grunted, his ears pricked forward. Trembling and sobbing, she tore off her T shirt, took up a sharp rock from the roadbed and raked her bare skin with her makeshift weapon. Dark blood welled up in long gashes along her arms, her rounded breasts, across her cheeks.

The gift is accepted. So be it.

The big cat whined his nostrils flaring with the scent of fresh blood, but still he hesitated. "Come on, I know you're hungry. Finish it."

Candace dropped the rock and chanted her own Give-away Song in answer to the ancestors. Her voice became more confident with each breath. The slopes of the mountains rang with her Death Song.

The night pulsed with power.

All the pain, all the torment and unfulfilled longings of her life, were focused and given a new purpose by her willing surrender. Taken and transformed by the spirits, in that moment out of time, the raw emotions of her soul became an act of deliverance – an act of power.

Candace looked up as the hunter sprang, but kept on singing. Her song blended with the cougar's scream. Sharp fangs bit into warm flesh. Long claws ripped at her exposed belly. The salty taste of her own blood was in her mouth, choking off breath. Pain, Oh, Mother Earth, Great Spirit, so much pain –

Death cannot be conquered, granddaughter. We all must die; that is the way of the Medicine. And when Death comes to you, embrace him like a lover. That is a woman's wisdom and the way to true freedom.

Candace raised her arms and grasped the cougar's powerful shoulders. Smooth silky fur rippled under her hands. She curled her fingers and felt them dig into hard muscular flesh. Ah, yes-s-s. Candace rocked her hips and wrapped her legs around him, pulling him closer.

The hunter sank his teeth into her throat. Her vision blurred. The song in her mind grew louder, matching its cadence to the pounding of her dying heart. Oh, how it hurt – oh, how sweet!

WHEN CANDACE AWOKE the world was a monochrome assortment of gray shapes in the pale dawn light. What a night, what crazy dreams she'd had. She closed her eyes, yawned and burrowed deeper into her nest of debris under the drooping cedar. Her belly was distended from her last meal; she felt lazy and content. Maybe she'd sleep a little longer before she finished her walk and caught a ride.

Nearly asleep, her sensitive nostrils suddenly picked out the odors of coyote piss and drying blood. Blood? Where? Candace's eyes flew open.

Protruding from a mound of dead leaves she could see a woman's half eaten arm bone. Pale bone showing through gnawed gray flesh, the fingers of the hand were curled into rigid claws. Her eyes riveted on the gruesome sight, she sprang to her feet. Walking over to the corpse she took a cautious sniff, her tail lashed in agitation.

Oh, Merciful Mother – it was her arm.

Crouched in a part of their bound soul she suddenly became aware of the frightened essence of a cougar – a young male, vibrant with life. He growled and watched her warily with feral glowing eyes. Panic twisted a knot in her gut. She opened her mouth to scream, but only a cat's terrified yowl choked out her constricted throat. Candace's essence shimmered with uncertainty. What had happened to her? Why couldn't she remember?

Wake up; this is a dream. Remember what you've been taught, stupid girl. You can get out – master your fear –

Calm yourselves, my children, the Earth Spirit said to them. *Your gift has been accepted, Warrior Woman. New Guardian of this land, we charge you and your soul mate with its care. Strength of the beast, intelligence of human woman, avatar who shares our power to walk between the worlds, we are pleased with you.*

Candace would have liked to ask the spirit more questions, but they were interrupted by the rumble of vehicles coming up the road.

Danger, the big cat warned.

Instinct blotting out other considerations, the cougar part of her leapt for a tall cedar. Claws digging into its bark the big cat scrambled for a thick branch in its concealing foliage.

From this high perch, Candace conveyed to her soul mate the deeper meaning of those human-made sounds. The cougar flattened upon the branch and glared at the large yellow logging truck rolling past. A convoy of other vehicles trailed in a fog of dust in its wake. Loggers, coming to cut more trees. And just behind them, the police and the government men were coming to arrest protesters and stop the blockade.

Tail lashing, Candace growled deep in her throat, wanting to sink her teeth into soft white flesh.

A hunter must learn patience, the cougar counseled.

When the convoy was only a faint murmur in the distance Candace urged climbing down, but the cougar's keen ears detected stealthy movement in the undergrowth. Someone else was approaching.

Sensitive nostrils caught the scent of wood smoke, marijuana and rancid sweat. The cougar side of her nature trembled, uncertain. Caution warred with the instinct to protect her kill from trespassers. Motionless, she waited, her lip curled back from long fangs in a silent snarl.

As the invaders drew closer the human woman recognized the familiar faces of Jonas and two other friends. Jonas was one of the main organizers of the blockade. He should be manning the line, defending the trees. Had he been so worried about her that he'd abandoned his post to follow her?

Jimmy's words abused her of that notion. "Oh, man. Jonas, we're nearly to the highway. Where is she? Has she escaped our conjuring?"

Jonas waved a hand in the direction of the mounded debris under a nearby tree. Jimmy and Roseanne stepped over to look. "She's right there."

Candace heard the sound of vomiting and a woman's startled sob. A note of awe coming into his voice, Jimmy said, "Oh, wow! When she ran away like that I thought it was game over."

A low mirthless laugh, then Jonas said, "Jimmy, Jimmy there was never any doubt of the outcome. I recognized the hunger to belong in her eyes the first time I met her. Seducing her and manipulating her into taking part in the ceremony was no true challenge of my power. She belongs to me – just as you do. Never forget that, cousin. Have more faith in future. We will save our land from being raped once again by the government and those apple Indians on the council."

Jimmy let out a nervous laugh. "I do have faith. Now that the old woman's dead, only you have the power to really stop those fuckers."

"Oh, Candi," Roseanne moaned. Her body trembling she stared transfixed at the remains half buried in the debris. "I'm so sorry. I didn't know – not all of it – oh, Candi –" Covering her face with her hands she broke out into loud sobbing.

A look of disgust distorting his handsome face, Jonas snapped, "Calm down, Roseanne. She isn't dead. And you're frightening the cat with your noise." He tried to put an arm about her shoulder, but she flinched away.

"Don't touch me, you murdering devil."

At mention of the cougar, Jimmy looked up, trying to spot Candace in the greenery. Their eyes met and his mouth fell open.

Turning away from the hysterical woman Jonas put a hand on his cousin's shoulder. Still mesmerized by the cougar, Jimmy let out a low whistle. "Oh, man, oh, man, you really did it."

Jonas's mouth molded itself into a hard line. "Damn you, Jimmy, never mind the cat. Leave her to me." He pointed with his chin to Roseanne. "There's some hash in my pack. Give her a bowl. Get her calmed down, before she spoils everything."

To add extra emphasis to his words, he gave his cousin a shove in Roseanne's direction. With one last look at the cougar, Jimmy put an arm around the crying woman's shoulders and led her away.

When all was quiet in the forest, the birds and tiny animals once more going about their daily routines, Jonas raised his hand and curled his fingers in command. "Come down. It's time for us to leave, Kitten."

The witch's tendril of power tried to coil itself about her, but the big cat snarled and batted it away.

Grandma Dorothy's ghost drifted out of the trees behind Jonas. A skeletal hand pointed to the half concealed medicine bundle he held cradled under his jacket. A luminous cord hung about the ghost's neck, binding the spirit both to the beloved medicine bundle and the witch.

You must stop him, Granddaughter, or I can never rest.

"Stop me, old woman?" Jonas barked a laugh, shaking his head. "No, no, she can't do that. She belongs to me, too. She is my most powerful weapon to save the trees."

Save the trees, but at what cost in misery for others? Is protecting our land your true motive, you bastard?

"Candi, Candi, don't be crude," Jonas chided. "Of course I want to protect our land and save the old growth trees. And you will help me. Just as you wanted all along."

Candace yowled, the pain of his betrayal like a blade stabbed in her heart. He had had the bundle all along, manipulating her, the family and her grandmother's ghost for his own ends.

Save the trees and make you a big chief; save the trees and give you power. That's what you really want, isn't it?

Had he killed Grandma Dorothy as well? Oh Great Spirit, had he coveted Cougar's power that much? This added revelation hit her like an axe blow, nearly dropping her from her perch.

Patience, the big cat murmured in her mind. *A hunter must let go hot anger. Not needed to bring down prey.*

Yes. You are right, soul brother. The cougar steadied, her claws biting deep into the branch upon which she sat.

Your trickery may have led me to take part in the ceremony that began the transformation, but we belong to the spirits of the land now. Not to you, Witch, Candace snarled.

"Candi, Candi, you're talking nonsense. Of course you are mine." He held up the medicine bundle. "As long as I have this and the ghost to do my bidding, you can't defy me. Don't even try."

Candace felt her blood run cold. He was right; no escape – no escape! Her soul mate, however, didn't agree and answered the witch with a cougar's deep-throated scream of challenge.

Jonas growled a curse. Eyes alight with anticipation, he smiled. "All right, we can do this the hard way if you like. Just remember that as Jimmy has already learned, and your cousin Roseanne soon will, pain comes to those who disobey me."

Jonas drew a knife from his jeans pocket and crossed to the corpse. Crouching, he raised the gnawed arm bone to show her, then severed one of its curled fingers. "With this I claim your soul. Flesh and spirit, breath and bone, you belong to me. There is no escape. You will come. And you will obey – oh yes, you will obey."

Run, granddaughter, the ghost cried. *You must not let him ensnare you with his power.*

Candace needed no further urging; she had already recognized the danger and conveyed the menace to her soul mate. Before Jonas had a chance to focus his power the cougar leapt from her branch to another racing through the forest canopy.

Tripping over tree roots, long hair snagging in the undergrowth, Jonas followed, cursing as he ran.

Candace thought she might escape, then she heard Jonas shout, "Come back or I will use my power to destroy her. Do you want your grandmother's spirit to be torn apart, never to find peace?"

Don't listen to him, my girl, run. Never mind me it doesn't matter what he does to me!

Ah, but it did matter – to her.

The cougar crouched on a thick branch above him and snarled, giving him an impressive look at her fangs.

The malicious laugh again, "You're a stubborn bitch, aren't you? But I like a challenge. I'm going to enjoy taming you, oh yes."

Gory talisman held tight in his clinched fist, Candace felt the witch's ghostly hands close about her throat and squeeze. Breath coming in ragged grunts, the cougar clung to the branch as the world before her eyes dimmed.

"Here pussy, pussy. Come, you can't fight me, pretty pussy."

Bad man. The cougar's voice was a feathery whisper in her mind.

No hope – no escape! She was going to die if she didn't surrender.

Courage, granddaughter. You have Cougar's power for your own. Fight the evil. Then she saw the ghost spring forward, loop its binding tether about the witch's neck and pull the cord tight.

Yes, my soul mate, he is a bad man, Candace said. *And for that reason we aren't going to give him time to strengthen his hold over us.*

With claws extended and teeth bared, the cougar sprang from the limb to fall upon her prey.

Guardians of the Bright Isles

Gran O'Cuinn brushed a tear from her eye and closed the cottage door gently, so as not to wake the children. Ah, her dear sweet grandbabies. Rory, only six, trying to be a man and help Turlouch with the nets. And her precious Ethne, only two – what would happen to her with no ma to care for her? She was so young – too young to hold all their futures in her wee white hand.

The old woman tightened the wool shawl about her shoulders and clumped in her high rubber boots down the steep trail to the beach. The light was no more than a rosy thread upon the eastern horizon. In the slippery places where sea mist pooled, she used her walking stick to steady herself. She had to tell Them.

Gray mists shrouded the water out in the cove, obscuring the Irish coast. From somewhere in the fog ahead the old woman heard seals barking and hastened in that direction. Coming round a spit of land, she saw dark heads popping in and out of the gray-green water. Closer into shore a few seals lounged on flat rocks exposed by the receding tide.

A seal barked an alarm, and those on the rocks waddled to the ocean and disappeared beneath the surface. The seals already in the water swam further away, then turned to watch her.

A mountain of a woman she brandished her stick, and shook it at them. "Stop your teasing, Ronfear. I know you're out there. Get over here, you sweet-talkin' devil, what are you and the old one going to do now?"

Gran's voice grew hoarse from shouting and tears of frustration streamed down her face, but the seals stayed well away from the beach and her wildly gesticulating stick.

"Here now, Mother O'Cuinn, what are you doin' out here so early of the mornin'?"

A man with curly dark hair, going white at the temples of his long weathered face, put out a hand to adjust the shawl that had slipped from her plump shoulder, then hastily jumped back as her stick whirled in his direction.

Recognizing him, she lowered the stick and glared. "You know very well, Turlouch O'Murchu, what I'm doin'. If Gormla Burke returns to the manor to claim her brother's property, she will send us all to sleep in ditches along the roads like tinkers. I know that evil woman. She hates us – and Them." Turning, she shook her stick again at the vanished seals.

"There now, everything will turn out well. No need to fear, ta' be sure." Making soothing noises, Turlouch took her hand and led her up the beach. When they reached the trail, he motioned for her to precede him. "Old Mother, you're a shiverin' like a leaf in the wind. You'll catch your death – and then what will the children do? Go on back before the little ones miss you. Have more faith. They will take care of us."

Assured that Gran was well on her way back to her cottage, Turlouch turned toward the small peer where several of his neighbors were getting ready for a day of fishing. Gulls wheeled and cried overhead. A dripping young man squatted in the bow of his motorboat when he arrived. Ignoring him, Turlouch retrieved his drying net from a nearby rack, heaved its mass onto the deck between the seats and climbed in.

"Coward."

Ronfear's eyes widened, then he laughed. Untying the mooring rope, he settled himself comfortably in the bow. The young man's long dark hair had been pulled back into a ponytail by a piece of ropy seaweed. He had enigmatic dark eyes and a high cheek-boned face with drooping brown mustaches. Stroking one end, he smiled. "Call me coward if you will, cousin, but I have no wish to spoil a beautiful morning."

Turlouch snorted a laugh of his own. "So, even one such as you tremble and duck under the waves at the thought of a lashing from Gran O'Cuinn's tongue." Still chuckling to himself, Turlouch started the engine and guided the vessel into the maze of tiny Seal islands that clustered between his home and the Irish coast.

The mist shredded in the morning breeze, the sun fanning out in a golden ribbon across the green water. When they could no longer be observed from either shore, Turlouch cut the engine and allowed the boat to drift near a small gravel beach. Ronfear jumped out and helped Turlouch guide the boat higher onto the shore.

An old man was waiting for them, gray hair flowing down his back in long ropy tangles, his face surprisingly youthful. A furred cloak about his shoulders, the thick-bodied elder sat cross-legged in a mound of dry seaweed, as regal as any king upon a golden throne. Turlouch bowed his head and squatted at his feet. Posting himself as sentry, Ronfear crouched near them to listen.

Bitterness colouring his voice, the old man said, "So, the Burke is dead."

Turlouch sighed. "Tis a great tragedy. The attack came on him sudden like – so they say. I'm sure he would have kept his promise, if he had lived a little longer. Though not a true one of us, he was a caring Guardian."

After a thoughtful pause, the Elder said, "Sudden like. Was his heart attack an undetected human weakness, or something more?"

A shiver ran down Turlouch's backbone. He shook his head, wanting to deny the threat to all of them the Elder's words implied. "Surely not, Elder. The Burke was well respected and loved –"

Ronfear snorted, interrupting. "And what of the fishermen living near Black Rock? They are angry when a seal steals some of their salmon, then shelters out of reach in the protected waters of the Burke's Wild-Life Sanctuary. One of them could have hired a Ban-Feasa to conjure for him –"

"Enough!" the Elder barked, making a cutting motion with his hand. Ronfear fell silent. Returning his attention to Turlouch, he asked, "What does Una say? Will the Burke's sister be returning?"

Turlouch shook his head. "Gormla, a pity about her. Such a beauty in her youth. Too bad her parents were talked into sending her abroad to that convent school."

"As if I would have let anything happen to her," Ronfear muttered. "She had been promised me."

Turlouch agreed, smiling. "Tis sure you would, I've no doubt – a handsome lad such as yourself. Turn any woman's head, not your fault at all. The sisters filled her pretty head with the notion that some of her own kin were soulless spawn of the devil." He held out his hands and shrugged. "And what could her aged mother do but go against tradition and name the brother to inherit. And then later to find out the poor man had been cursed and was unable to sire children – a tragedy for us all, to be sure."

Still with a thoughtful look in his eye, the Elder nodded. "Though claiming her power comes from her god, Gormla Burke is a Ban-Feasa nonetheless. I always wondered if she had a hand in that conjuring. But if she were to return now..."

"You needn't fear. I think maybe she is afraid of you, Elder. My cousin Una working at the manor said Gormla didn't come home, even for her brother's funeral."

The Elder's cutting gesture again, "The Burke is gone. The future is what I must focus my power upon now. If we are forced to abandon our charge, I fear the evil threatening the coasts of Eire, and Mother Ocean will only worsen."

Turlouch gave the Elder an apologetic look, then turned to Ronfear and winked. "Una says it is the Burke's niece Mara who was written up in the will to inherit."

Ronfear's white teeth flashed in a winning smile. "I think I remember her, a lovely lass. The Burke used to bring her with him to the Bright Isle on occasion." He fingered his long mustache. "Now that she is a woman grown, I think I will enjoy making her acquaintance."

The Elder frowned and reminded them. "Gormla's daughter hasn't visited since she was twelve or thirteen. The mother has had plenty of time to infect her child with her venom. I agree 'twill be necessary for you to ensure she doesn't sell our sanctuary, but something more than your handsome face may be needed to achieve her compliance."

Ronfear's smile widened. "Never fear, father, my handsome face is magic enough to get what I want from any woman."

Without warning the Elder rose with a growl, looming over his son in a show of dominance. Ronfear's expression soured, but as the Elder's eyes continued to bore into him, he reluctantly sighed and bowed his head in submission. "I will do what is necessary never fear."

"See that you do."

Shivers running down his spine, Turlouch protested in a quavering voice, "Oh surely Miss Mara will do right by us. She is a fine woman, Una says."

The Elder grunted, unconvinced. "When does she return from Galway?"

"Tomorrow, Una thinks," Turlouch said.

An unspoken communication passed between father and son, then the Elder strode off down the shore to disappear among the rocks and mist. Turlouch rose and stared after him, a knot of fear twisted in his gut.

Ronfear put a hand on his shoulder. “Come, cousin, I will help you with the boat before I leave to find my breakfast.”

Together the two men walk back to Turlouch’s skiff and launched it into the water. Turlouch paused before starting the motor.“I know you, or the Elder, tried a conjuring on Gormla – and it failed. You won’t hurt Miss Mara will you?”

Ronfear’s handsome face grew thoughtful. “We know so little of the world beyond these isles. Perhaps, it was a mistake to try and force Gormla to keep her part in the ancient bargain. If I had had more time – but father...”

Echoing the Elder’s cutting motion with his hand, Ronfear puffed out his breath in a frustrated huff. Then he flashed his winning smile again and pushed the boat into deeper water. “Don’t look so worried, Cousin. I have no desire to have a slave. “A warm lusty lover would be far more to my liking.”

Unable to believe him, but fearing to offend, Turlouch dropped his eyes and started the engine. When he looked up Ronfear was gone. Suppressing a shudder, Turlouch guided the boat out into the channel. “But on the other hand, me lad, in spite of your soothing words to me, you’ll obey the Elder and do what is necessary, no matter the cost to the woman.”

MARA’S NEW INHERITANCE wasn’t filling her heart with joy. In fact, it was turning out to be more trouble than it was worth, according to her fiancé Adam. The Burke manor was old, its history going back several centuries. It wasn’t over large and due to its owner’s financial troubles in recent years looked, and was, quite run down. There was a main house up on the cliff overlooking the ocean. Around the house were clustered a few out buildings, some trees and an overgrown garden that had gone to seed. A small peer and boathouse huddled on the rocky shore below the cliff.

Alone in her uncle’s library Mara listened without interest to her fiancé Adam talking on the hall telephone. In the funereal silence of the house his voice was a jarring reminder of the world they’d left behind in Boston.

Out across the jade green ocean the sky was awash with mauve, cool grays, and coral. Near the horizon the cliffs of a rocky island, that was also part of her inheritance, blazed like fire in the setting sun. In the tiny cove that faced the house, the island's whitewashed cottages with their thatched roofs had turned cream and gold in the waning glow. Inis Gheal it was called in Irish, or Bright Island in English.

Leaning her cheek against the cool glass of the window, she could almost hear the soft-spoken people and smell the pungent odors of fish, burning peat, and rotting seaweed that clung to everything. Wispy hair curling about a pink face, his round body quivering with excitement, how uncle's green eyes used to sparkle when he talked about the island – and the seals. It was like he knew a secret about them that no one else knew.

There'd been a time when Mara would have given anything to know that secret, but after her father's death, her mother had refused to allow her to visit Uncle Seamas on her own. She was devastated at first, then her friends, her studies at high school and later university occupied all her time. Though she'd made a half-hearted effort to keep in touch with her uncle as an adult, Seamas's fatal illness and her inheritance had come as a total surprise.

While lost in her reverie the sun had set; Inis Gheal was no more than a dark shadow floating upon a gray sea. Its enchanting beauty was gone, like the man who had showed her its wonders. Her vision blurred, tears running down her cheeks. The world felt like a darker place for his absence.

"Mara?"

Adam stood in the doorway, his face wearing a distracted look. Running a hand through his thinning hair, he peered into the dim interior of the library. Mara was grateful he couldn't see her face; she was just a dark silhouette against the window.

"Mara?"

"I'm all right Adam. What is it?"

He frowned, then came over to her and put an arm loosely about her shoulder. His lips brushed hers, then he stepped back to study her better. "Oh, honey, crying again?"

Mara yearned to fall into his arms and sob her heart out, but past experience had taught her the wisdom of restraint. He was uncomfortable with strong emotional displays.

"Honey, I know he was your favorite uncle and all that, but you've got to let go of the past and be reasonable."

Be reasonable. Stepping away from him, Mara walked to the large mahogany desk. Pulling out a tissue from her purse, she blew her nose. More composed, she flicked on the desk lamp and turned to face him. "Adam, can't you let it alone? Uncle Seamas is barely cold in the ground. Selling Inis Gheal is a major decision; I don't want to rush it."

Adam let out a long-suffering sigh and flopped into an over-stuffed leather chair. "Mara, look, I know we've been over this, time and time again, since the funeral. But you're going to have to make some compromises. I'm sure you would like to boast to your colleagues that you've inherited a 'grand old Irish manor.' But the bottom line is, you can't afford the house and grounds – unless you sell the island. And the decision isn't going to get any easier the longer you wait."

Like me the love of these isles is in your blood, girl, never forget that. And someday you will have to care for, and protect them as I do. Mara stifled a shiver as the memory of her uncle's prediction echoed anew in her mind's ear.

"Damn it, Adam, that isn't fair!" Mara cried, feeling tears threatening again. "I have no intention of 'boasting' to anyone – about anything. But the situation is – complicated –"

"Oh, please, not that again. The Gaelic clan tradition died out centuries ago. There are only a few old people and children left on the island anyway. Isn't it time their families took some responsibility for their indigent relatives, instead of expecting them to live off Seamas Burke's charity?"

"Those people aren't charity cases. They fish and –"

He held up a placating hand. "OK, OK, but the point is still, that the income from the rents doesn't cover the cost of the caretakers salaries, the taxes and the manor's maintenance. Selling the property on Inis Gheal to people looking for summer homes is the only way to make the manor cost efficient."

Mara opened her mouth to argue further, then noticed Una MacCarthaigh, standing in the doorway. A plump woman with her gray hair twisted in a knot at the nape of her neck, Una had been cook and housekeeper at the manor since Mara's childhood.

Pointedly ignoring Adam, Una focused her watery blue eyes on Mara, and asked, "Excuse me, dinner is ready, Miss Mara. Would you be a wantin' it now?"

AFTER THE CARETAKERS had retired, Mara tiptoed into Adam's bedroom. Dark mahogany furniture and roses on the wallpaper, the room was cool, the lacy curtain across the open window billowing like a sail. From the darkness beyond came the hiss of the surf along the shingle. Crossing to the window, she pulled it closed, then turned at a footstep behind her.

Finished in the bath down the hall, Adam crossed to his packed bag and slipped the shaving kit inside. Then as if noticing her for the first time, he feigned surprise. A smile played about the corners of his mouth. "Ah-ha, and just what would you be doing in here, hmm?" She gave him a wink, her own smile an open invitation.

"Aren't you worried about the gossip Una might spread? Unmarried heiress, dressed only in her nightgown, caught sneaking into a man's room in the night?"

Mara kissed him. "I don't care what she thinks or says. I'm not planning to live here, after all. The pretense of sleeping in separate rooms was mama's stupid idea – to protect my reputation – not mine. Do you have to go?"

Adam brushed past her, sat down on the bed and took off his slippers before answering. "Yes I have to go."

Mara frowned and collapsed onto the bed beside him, their bodies touching. "How long will you be gone?"

Adam sighed. "I don't know. Laurence wants me to go to the meeting with him in New York. Then, I may have to fly to Brazil." Adam put his arm around her shoulder and she rested her head on his chest.

"I'm going to miss you."

He gave her a squeeze and stroked her dark auburn hair. "You could fly to Boston and wait for me there. Don't you have things to do before your classes start?"

Reluctantly, she nodded. Adam kissed her hair and wrapped his arms a little tighter around her. Mara relaxed into his caress. Adam was a good man. Oh he could be insensitive at times, when he was immersed in his business projects, but as her mother kept assuring her, he would make a good provider.

She was a lucky woman – everyone said so.

"Laurence knows someone in real estate in Galway. On my next trip to Dublin I can schedule time to come here and take care of things – maybe make us a nice little nest egg."

When they were married in a few months, he would naturally assume such distasteful chores, chores for which she had no liking or ability. Why not let him do this for her – as an expression of his love now?

"Adam? Have you been conspiring with mama again?"

He frowned, disconcerted by her change of topic. "Don't be so suspicious. We're not plotting behind your back. But she did call while you were in the bath – sorry if I forgot to mention it." Then returning to his topic, he said, "Her call is beside the point. Like you, I have problems following her convoluted reasoning – evil fairies out to get her. But on the other hand, we both agree that you should go home."

Mara hesitated, thinking, then said, "Your arguments seems reasonable – but I think Uncle Seamas would be so disappointed in me if I abandoned my responsibilities to another. Let me think about it for a while longer, OK?"

Jaw tight, he climbed into the bed behind her. "I can see there's no reasoning with you. Do what you want, then."

For a moment her eyes flashed with anger, then she sighed and lay down beside him. There was no point in arguing with him; he wasn't Irish. He didn't – and maybe couldn't understand. To him, selling the island was just a logical business decision.

He smelled of soap and spicy aftershave. Moving closer, Mara slipped her hand under the waistband of his pajamas, letting it come to rest in the thatch of curly hair at his crotch. Cupping his shaft she stroked him, inviting more intimacy. She was looking forward to their wedding, when she could at last throw away her birth control pills.

Gently, but firmly, he took her hand away. "Not now, Mara, I've got a car coming to pick me up at six. I have to get some sleep."

Determined not to let him know how he'd hurt her, she pulled back the blanket and stood. "Well I guess I'll go then." Hand on the door she took a deep breath and said without a tremor, "Have a safe trip. Call me tomorrow when you get in. Good night."

His sleepy voice floated out to her from the darkness. "I will. Good night, love. Come back to Boston soon, okay?"

As the door closed behind her, Mara heard his quiet snoring falling into rhythm with the waves on the beach below. Tears pooled in the corners of her eyes as she felt her way down the dim corridor to her own room.

Unable to sleep, she lay with the down comforter pulled up to her neck and listened to the crash and hiss of the waves against the beach below her window. Normally those sounds would sooth and put her to sleep, too, but not that night.

Mara stared at the grey ceiling until she couldn't stand it anymore. In the bathroom down the hall was the bottle of sedatives that Uncle Seamas's doctor had prescribed for her – should she need them.

On her way back to bed, the seals sounded so near that she detoured to look out the window. The moon had risen behind the house. At the water's edge the surf foamed, leaving trails of silver froth along the gravel. Were those dark forms in the water seals or just rocks? It was impossible to tell in the dim light.

Then, was that a naked man she saw just stepping out of the surf? Yes, it was. But who on earth would be swimming in that cold water in the middle of the night? A monochrome figure of light and shadow, he stood looking up at her window. The man couldn't possibly see her, and yet she had the bizarre feeling that he was aware of her regard.

For just a moment, a pendant of some kind hanging around his neck flashed silver in the moonlight, then the light was gone. Mara couldn't see him clearly, the moon kept ducking behind the clouds, but the caretaker, Sean MacCarthaigh, never struck her as the type to bathe nude in the sea.

Then, the overwhelming urge to go down and walk with this stranger popped into her mind. Her breath quickening, she yearned to let him hold her and kiss away her grief and loneliness. She imagined his hands, strong and warm, caressing the most sensitive parts of her body, and his lips, tasting of salt, upon hers, his tongue gently, but insistently forcing them apart to receive his kisses. The sensation was so vivid, it seemed as if he stood in the room beside her.

Suddenly afraid, Mara slammed the window shut and backed hurriedly away, letting the curtain fall into place. Crawling between the sheets, she huddled with her face turned to the wall and pulled the comforter tight about her.

"Saints preserve us! Maybe there is more to mama's warnings than superstitious nonsense. Maybe – God, Mara, it's only an intruder down there not some evil fairy..."

But on the other hand, it was a private beach; she'd better warn Sean to watch out for the fellow in the morning.

MARA HEARD ADAM GETTING ready to leave, just after dawn. She supposed she ought to have made the effort, but she just couldn't summon the energy to crawl out of her warm bed to say good-bye. And besides, why did *she* always have to make the first move for reconciliation? He could have at least come in to give her a kiss. Pulling the sea-green comforter more securely about her shoulders, she forced herself to go back to sleep.

At last the smell of fresh baking wafted up the stairs and forced her to pay attention to her empty stomach. Mara remembered that smell from her childhood. Like an excited child anticipating a treat, she dressed in jeans and a flannel shirt, and hurried down to the kitchen. Then, feeling unexpectedly shy, she lingered in the doorway, unsure of her welcome.

Una was standing by the stove, stirring a big pot of something that smelled wonderful. Her husband Sean was sitting at the table, a cup of tea at his elbow and the morning paper spread out in front of him. Sean was a burly man with a rumpled thatch of gray hair and the bulging muscles of a man half his age.

Turning a page, Sean looked up, and when he saw her he motioned her over. Smiling, Mara pulled out a chair and joined him. Una poured her tea and sat a plate on the table between them. Spiced with ginger and cinnamon, the molasses soda-bread was as good as she recalled.

"Mmm, treacle farl. No one makes it better than you, Una. This was always my favourite when I visited as a girl. Did you remember how I loved it and make it special for me?"

Una set down a plate of bacon and eggs at her elbow and smiled. "Ta be sure I'm rememberin' Miss Mara."

Sean seemed impatient to return to his paper, so Mara concentrated on devouring the breakfast Una had made for her. Then, her eye caught sight of a headline about a break in to a summer home. Suddenly reminded of last night's nude swimmer, she sat down her cup and asked, "Sean, I saw a man on the beach last night. Is there someone else staying here?"

Sean looked over the edge of his paper. At the stove Una dropped her spoon with a clang. She bent to pick it up, and as she straightens she and Sean exchanged looks. Without a word, Una went to the sink and washed off the spoon.

Now that she had their undivided attention, Mara's stomach felt queasy – like she'd said something she shouldn't.

"There's no one else here," Sean said. "Are you sure you saw someone?"

Shrugging, she picked up her tea, trying to act casual. "No, I'm not sure. It was probably just a trick of the light."

The MacCarthaighs exchanged looks again, then Sean said, "I'll keep my eyes open, and if there is someone hanging around, I'll send him on his way, so don't worry."

Mara nodded, relieved to be done with the subject. But the earlier atmosphere of camaraderie between them had been spoiled. Swallowing hard to choke down her tears, Mara put down her cup with an unsteady hand, and asked, "Sean, are you busy today?"

"Not over much, why?"

"I-I'd like to go over to Inis Gheal. Could you take me?"

Studying her carefully, he took a sip of his tea before answering. "Are you going to tell them so soon then? Your man said you might be leaving us in a day or two."

Both embarrassed and angry, Mara felt the blood heat her cheeks. "Oh he did, did he?" And, Una must have been listening by the library door last night, as she'd suspected. "I don't know what I'm going to do about the estate. Right now, I just want to see the island again – and maybe talk to Old Gran O'Cuinn, if she's still alive."

He nodded. "She is. Well, I have to take some supplies he ordered, to Turlouch O'Murchu some time this week. Today's as good a day as any."

From her place by the stove Una said in a brittle voice, "I know old Mr. Burke didn't leave you much money. But surely before he died your uncle told you about the Good People? Isn't that why he left you his property? Inis Gheal is special; it must be kept safe. Money ain't everything – where will they go if you sell?"

Una herself had grown up on the island, living there, until she married Sean and came to work at the manor. Guilt spurring her, Mara said in a rush, "I know, Una, I don't want to sell the island; I'm trying to think of something to make it all work out."

Folding the paper with a snap, Sean growled, "Una, enough. Miss Mara will do the best for us she can, so stop badgering her."

Mara gave him a grateful look, wishing she had the same confidence in herself. Turning back to her, he said, "I have a few things to do first. Can you be ready to go in about an hour?" Una scowled at them both, but remains silent.

Returning to the library Mara decided that while she waited she might as well continue working on Seamas's papers. Engrossed in a document some time later, she jumped when the phone unexpectedly rang. Thinking it might be Adam, she reached across the desk for it.

"Hello."

"Mara, is that you dear?"

"Oh, hi, Mama. Why are you calling so early?"

"Do I need a reason to talk to my daughter?"

Mara sighed, tapping her pencil impatiently. She didn't have time for her mother now – she should have let Una answer it; it was her home after all. "No, of course not, mama. It's just I thought you hate spending money on Trans-Atlantic calls."

"I do. But since I never hear from you otherwise, I guess I will have to spend some of my widow's pension and make the effort for both of us."

Mara rolled her eyes. In her mind's eye she could see her mother, sitting in her over-stuffed easy chair, the TV talking to itself in the corner of her cluttered living room. With snapping green eyes and a pale heart-shaped face, Gormla had been a beauty once and in spite of the extra weight she carried, she was still vain about her looks. In her youth she'd had stunning red hair, but the effect of the red dye she now used to hide the grey lent her permed hair an artificial pink tinge. Mara would never dare tell her so, however. she'd never hear the end of it if she did."You could have just waited to talk to me till I got home, mama, and saved your money."

"Or you could call your mother once in a while."

"Yes, mama."

"And, since you brought the subject up, when are you and Adam coming home?"

"Adam left for Boston this morning. I'm not sure when I'm coming back. There is still so much to do here to get uncle's affairs in order –"

"What! I told him – you mean to tell me that Adam left you alone there?"

Mara let out another long-suffering sigh. "I'm a big girl, Mama. I don't need Adam to hold my hand. And besides, I'm hardly alone. Sean and Una are here."

Nearly frantic with desperation, Gormla cried, "You would be better off alone, than staying there with those people. Una is one of them! Mara, tell me true. Are you still wearing the necklace I gave you?"

Without thinking, Mara raised her free hand to touch the saint's medallion on a gold chain about her throat. It had been a parting gift from her mother. Gormla claimed it had been blessed by a priest and would protect her from evil. "Yes, Mama. I am still wearing the medal – and I won't take it off till I'm back in Boston like you made me promise."

"Saints be praised, good." Gormla paused in her rant, then began a new, "My girl, you have to get out of that house – Ireland – it isn't safe for you there –"

"What? Losing faith in your talisman?"

"None of your smart mouth, girl!" Gormla shouted into the phone. "This is serious. Your immortal soul will be lost if you are tempted by their conjuring. You are in danger, I tell you."

Mara jerked the phone away from her ear and scowled. When her mother paused for breath, she said, "Stop worrying I'll be home in a few days, as soon as I get things sorted out. Nothing's going to happen to me. No evil fairies or hobgoblins are going to kidnap me. I'll be fine. Stop worrying."

"Mara, I know you think this is all a joke, that I'm growing senile, but I'm perfectly sane. You are in danger if you stay there. Please come back to Boston. Leave today."

"All right, I'll leave. As soon as you come here to do the work needed to get uncle's tangled legal affairs in order. Shall I expect you on the next plane?"

There was a long silence on her mother's end of the line, finally Gormla said in a tight voice, "You know I can't. They will kill me."

Mara laughed. "Right, the evil fairies. Bye, Mama, see you soon." Still chuckling to herself, Mara hung up the phone, grabbed her jacket off the chair and headed for the peer.

WHEN MARA ARRIVED AT the dock, Sean was just pouring petrol into the boat's tank. She grabbed a lifejacket from the rack inside the boathouse and joined him. Settling herself in the bow, she gathered her courage and asked the question that she couldn't get out of her mind since Una's outburst.

"Sean? Una acts like there's some big secret about Inis Gheal that I should know, but I can't recall my uncle telling me anything special. He did a lot of babbling near the end. But it was just the crazy talk of a sick old man on high doses of pain medication—nothing more, surely. Do *you* know what she's talking about?"

Sean glanced up from checking the level of petrol flowing into the tank but didn't answer. Turning back to the engine, he capped the tank and stowed the can in a locker. "Una can be a superstitious old woman at times. Don't pay her any mind. On the subject of Inis Gheal and the Seal Islands, she's as crazy as the rest of them out there. It's time they all woke up and realized what century they're living in. Maybe it would be the best thing for all of them if you *did* sell."

Mara wanted to ask more, but he terminated their conversation by starting the motor, and expertly guided them out into the bay.

As the boat neared Inis Gheal, the dark heads of gray seals began to pop in and out of sight among the waves. Gulls screaming overhead, wind blowing her hair, jade green water whipped to white froth in their wake, Mara felt the knot of tension in her stomach unwind for the first time in days.

In the sheltered cove on the lee side of the island, Sean slid the motorboat alongside a weathered peer. He hopped out while she held the boat steady and moored it to a large cleat. Mara smiled and joined him on the dock. "That was wonderful, Sean. I haven't enjoyed anything so much in a long time. On our way back I'd like a turn at the tiller. I believe I can still recall my uncle's lessons well enough to get us home."

Sean grunted and picked up a large sack and balanced it on his shoulder. "Best if you wait till I have time to look at the engine first. It's been giving me a bit of trouble lately." Then without waiting for her reply, he started climbing the trail.

About halfway up the cliff Mara paused to catch her breath, and happened to glance down into the cove. To her surprise, she saw a man in a long grey coat sitting cross-legged on the peer looking up at them. Where had he come from? She would have noticed him if he'd been there when they moored the boat – she was sure of it. From her position high on the trail, Mara couldn't see him clearly. But with his long dark ponytail, he didn't seem to her like a local. Giving the stranger one last glance over her shoulder, Mara hurried to catch up with Sean.

"Sean, who is that down in the cove? Do you know?"

Turning, he shaded his eyes with his free hand and looked where she was pointing. His expression darkened, and then he muttered a curse under his breath. "That one. Never mind about him, Miss Mara."

His reply had been curt, as if scolding an unruly child. Mara's mouth thinned into an angry line. Did he treat Una so harshly when no one was around? Macho bastard, damn him! Turning away while she calmed down, Mara glanced down at the cove again, but the man had disappeared.

Feeling suddenly uneasy as she recalled last night's intruder, Mara decided to risk irritating Sean further by pressing him for more details about the stranger. Hurrying to catch up with him again, she laid a hand on his shoulder, forcing him to stop and look at her. "Who *is* he, Sean? Could he be the intruder I saw last night on the beach?"

Sullen now, he muttered, "Could be – I don't know. If he has a name, I've never heard it. But he does live round here right enough."

"On Inis Gheal?"

"I don't know where he lives. He comes and goes as he pleases."

Mara glared, her temper close to igniting. Why was he being so evasive?

Sean must have read her thoughts from her expression, because he muttered, "I don't know. Even after being married to Una for more than twenty years, they still call me, 'the northern man' and keep their secrets. He had a woman on the island for a time, but she died a year back in a car accident near Galway. He's got a couple of kids by her – comes round to see them every once in a while. But he don't do a lick of work to support them. The good-for-nothing leaves their grandmother to take care of them on her own.

That's all I know." Sean closed his mouth tight and continued walking, leaving a frustrated Mara to trail in his wake.

As they reached the settlement, the smells of peat smoke and frying potatoes wafted out to greet them. Mara sighed with delight. The pungent smell of burning peat was one of the things about Ireland she missed most – there was nothing like it. And, just as she'd pictured her in her mind, Gran O'Cuinn was sitting on the stoop outside her cottage, a basket of wool by her feet, her knitting needles flying.

Gran was a large and imposing woman, her white hair pulled into a bun, her long skirt neatly tucked to cover her legs, she had a dark woolen shawl draped over her shoulders. Seeing them approach, her face creased into a thousand laugh-lines.

"Mara, mo cushla, conas ta tu? Come sit beside me; I was hoping you'd come to see me before you went back to Americay." Mara grinned and sat herself at the ancient's feet, just like in the old days.

Before they became too engrossed in their talk, Sean cleared his throat. "I got to take this stuff to Turlouch; when would you like me to come back for you, Mrs. Bensen?"

Mrs. Bensen? He must really be annoyed with her to revert to such formalities. Or maybe he was just trying to preserve her reputation. The tantalizing gossip that she had arrived at her uncle's sick bed with no chaperone and a man not related to her in tow, must have reached even to this isolated island. "Later this afternoon, if you please. I want to visit with Gran and maybe walk around the island for a time before going back."

Sean grunted, bobbed his head to the old woman and headed towards a cluster of cottages at the far end of the settlement.

It didn't take long before Mara and Gran were joined by many of the community's inhabitants. The children were shy, but stared curiously when they thought she wasn't looking. The men and women offered their condolences, but Mara could see the fear in their eyes. Suddenly reticent around them, she wondered why she'd come. She wasn't Seamas's favorite niece any more. No, she was a woman who had the power to change their way of life forever.

It had been a mistake to come here. Maybe she should let Adam handle things and sell. Why had she been so stupid – think it would be like before? Furious with herself, and her dead uncle for putting her in this awkward position, she wished she could call Sean back to rescue her. Hadn't she told Uncle Seamas years ago she had a new life in America? She didn't want this responsibility – he'd been unfair to expect so much of her.

And if not you, my girl, then who? Gormla? She failed us once. There is only you. A shiver ran down her backbone as Seamas's ghost repeated his dying words next to her ear. Mara waved a hand as if swatting at a fly. No more. She didn't want to listen

As if aware of her growing discomfort, Gran laid a reassuring hand on her arm.

Startled, Mara turned to her. "God bless you, child, I'm so glad to see you. We've missed you. When are you coming back to live in the manor?"

Mara flushed. "Gran, I'm sorry. I have no plans to live in Ireland. I have a good job in Boston – and I'm getting married in the autumn."

Gran seemed upset by her words. Oops, maybe she shouldn't have said that about getting married.

"Ah, I am sorry to hear that. Is your life good over there in Americay, then?"

Was it? Mara had thought so. Now, however, she wasn't sure. But she wasn't a girl anymore – she had a fiancé, a career – and, and, someday soon they'd have children to fill up that one empty spot in her world. Her tone defensive even to her own ears, Mara said, "Yes, I have a good life in Boston. I'm very happy there."

Gran studied her carefully, then nodded. "Good on you then. God Bless you, child." Tucking her knitting back into its basket, she rose and motioned for Mara and the other women to follow her into the cottage. "Let's have some tea."

Irish hospitality being a grand old tradition, Mara was also served fried potatoes, fish and hot-from-the-oven soda-bread. Feeling over full and looking for a polite way to excuse herself from Gran and her neighbors, Mara glanced out the cottage window and saw the gray-coated stranger, heading up the trail.

His face was pleasing, but Mara wouldn't have called him handsome. Still, there was something about him that caught her eye and made her heart flutter. His eyes were a soft brown. His cheekbones high, his nose well formed. In the style more popular in centuries past, he had a long drooping mustache that curved around full, sensual lips. He was carrying a roughly made willow basket over one arm and when he noticed Mara watching him, he smiled, displaying fine white teeth.

"Gran, who is that coming?"

The women fell silent, staring out the open door. No one answered her question. Then, the stranger was in the doorway. Bowing to Gran O'Cuinn, the eldest woman present, he proffered his basket to his host. "Old one, I've brought you some sea-lettuce and fish from the Seal Isles."

He was speaking English – for her benefit no doubt. Everyone else in the cottage spoke fluent Irish. Though his voice was melodic, Mara couldn't place his accent.

Gran took the basket, and thanked him. When he made no move to leave, she offered him tea from the kettle simmering on the stove. He nodded his thanks, grabbed a stool, and brought it over to sit beside Mara. Gran scowled as she set a cup of steaming tea in front of him.

Blowing away the steam, he took a loud slurp. "Ah, tea. A delicious drink – very stimulating." He gave Mara a wink. "Don't you agree?"

"I guess so."

The cottage was unnaturally silent. Mara glanced around the room, hoping someone would clue her in... but the women wouldn't meet her eye, or look at the newcomer. To her left, one of Gran's neighbours clutched her rosary and scowled. Gran on the other hand somehow managed to look both relieved and smug at the same time. The rest of the women clustered around the kitchen table, looked as if they'd rather be anywhere else at that moment.

When the stranger finished his tea, Gran folded her arms across her ample chest and fixed him with her, "Give me no nonsense" look. "I've been wanting to talk to you – which I believe you know. You have been avoiding me, Ronfear."

"Not true, Old Mother. I had no idea or I would have come sooner, to be sure."

Gran snorted, not believing a word. "Then why are you here, bringing me a gift, if you were not afraid I would be cross with you, eh?

The stranger's luminous dark eyes were suddenly moist with unshed tears. "Cross with me? I'm sure I can't imagine why you would be cross with me. I came with my gift, because I know how much you would enjoy it for your supper, Old Mother." He offered her a tentative smile. "What would you like to talk to me about? I am listening."

Gran sipped her tea watching him without comment till the smile wavered and disappeared.. "Made my old woman's heart tremble with worry, you did. But what I wanted to say is of no importance now – and you know that too, don't you?"

Ronfear dropped his eyes and shifted his weight nervously on the stool. Then turning to Mara is mood brightened once more. Looking into her eyes, he smiled, and said, "But since I'm here, and you have naught of importance to say to me, perhaps this pretty lady is tired of sitting and would like to take a walk with me?"

Startled, Mara blinked. Ronfear's smile widened. He had canine teeth that were more prominent than usual. Uncertain what to do next, Mara glanced at Gran her eyes asking if she should go with this stranger.

Gran nodded her approval. "Go if you like. Our Ronfear may lack the polish of a Boston man, but no harm will come to you on this island. I promise you that, my girl."

Feeling intrigued and a bit daring, Mara shrugged and stood. Addressing the room without looking at anyone, she announced, "I was planning on taking a walk anyway." Then giving Ronfear a tentative smile of her own, she added, "Thanks for the offer."

Ronfear laughed softly, pushed the stool away from the table and stood, offering his hand. "Come then. I will take you to the headland where you can look out over the ocean – all the way to America."

As they were leaving, Gran's voice stopped them. "Ronfear, remember and have a care. This young woman will marry soon."

"Will she now?"

Ronfear and Gran exchanged looks, then he said something in Gaelic that Mara couldn't understand. Scowling, Gran's reply was curt. He seemed amused and gave Mara another wink. Then at an angry growl from Gran he sobered and turned back to her. "I will keep your words in mind. I have a long memory as you know, Old Mother. I've never forgotten what was promised, and what is owing."

Sensing the undercurrents swirling about in the cottage, Mara glanced from one woman's face to the other. What was she missing? Would they tell her if she asked? Their behavior made Mara nervous. Perhaps she should make some excuse and decline the offer of a walk. But Ronfear gave her no time to change her mind. Taking her hand firmly in his own, he led her out the door into the watery sunshine.

INIS GHEAL WASN'T A big island – only a few miles in any one direction. Exposed to the Atlantic, it had an austere beauty. The essence of rock, water and wind, that was the magic of the Bright Isle. Few trees grew there. And the few that did manage to survive the winter gales, were stunted things that hid in sheltered crannies among the rocks or in the coves along the lee shore. Green grass, pale lichens and mosses were everywhere, and wild flowers speckled the land in summer. Remote, captivating, Mara could feel its enchantment, melting away her resistance to its primal allure. What did she have in America to compare with this? How could she ever bare to leave Inis Gheal and the manor again? Why had she ever left?

They walked silently, side-by-side where the trail permitted, but never touching. Both seem content to feel the sun on their backs and smell the salt tang in the air. He was an excellent companion for such a stroll. He never distracted her with useless chatter.

Finally tired of the treadmill of her own thoughts, she ventured, "I think I heard Gran call you Ronfear. Is that your name?"

"That is what some here call me."

"That's a rather ambiguous answer."

Ronfear took her hand. "Don't look so worried, mo chara. I've been called Ronfear by the people of this island for so long I answer to no other."

The Fairy Folk never give mortals their true name, my girl, lest we take advantage of them. For with a creature's true name comes a magical power over them that can be used for good or ill. The memory of Uncle Seamas's words made her shiver.

Determined not to let her companion know how much he disturbed her, Mara slipped her hand out of his. "Ronfear. That's a Gaelic word isn't it?"

"It's two words actually. Together they mean, Seal Man."

"You mean they think you're a selkie?""

"Yes."

Mara stared openmouthed, then laughed. "Jesus, Mary and Joseph, you're joking right?"

He watched her solemnly for a moment, then laughed along with her. "The folk here have their strange notions, to be sure."

At the headland Mara gazed out across the Atlantic, marveling. "It's so vast," she murmured. "It makes me feel insignificant and when the wind blows, so lonely."

"Lonely? What an odd notion," Ronfear said. "Does the wind never speak of joyous things to you?"

"No." Deciding to humor him, she asked, "What does the wind say to *you*?"

He chuckled and took back her hand. "You are toying with me, mo chara, I can see it in your eyes. But no matter. There are many Winds and they can teach you."

What was that around his neck? Ah, a shell pendant. For just a moment it flashed silver in the sunlight, then he moved, concealing its light once more. Mara couldn't help smiling; his good humor was contagious. Whom was toying with whom, she wondered.

"Oh? Go on. Tell me more."

"Well, there is the cold Blue Wind that sings of grief and longing—that one, you hear too well. Then there is the Green Wind whose soft breath brings joy. There is the Red Wind of war and the Speckled Wind that shares the news from afar. All about us the Winds are singing, just waiting for you to join your voice to their song."

"I wish it were that simple for me."

Following her mood, Ronfear sobered. "With me by your side, it could be, my heart, truly it could." As if in agreement, the wind gusted, tangling in their hair. Then in the next breath, it died to a soft moan.

Was he making a pass? The isolated spot, the wind and the man beside her, all of it was getting far too weird for her liking. "I should go back now. Sean will be coming for me soon."

"You are cold, mo chara." Coming up behind her, Ronfear pulled her into the shelter of his embrace. And to her shame, she found his touch a welcome balm to her battered soul.

Why couldn't it be Adam here with me instead of a stranger? Why doesn't Adam ever hold me like this – oh why?

"Pretty Mara, with the sea-green eyes," Ronfear murmured. The sweet cadence of his voice seemed to weave an enchantment about them. "Is the love of these islands in your blood, as it is in mine?"

Mara turned, searching his face. Her mouth quivered and tears pooled in the corners of her eyes. "My uncle used to ask me that. Did you know him?"

"I knew him. He was a fine man. He was very protective of the sea and its peoples – as am I. We talked many times over the years."

She sniffed, determined not to embarrass herself further in front of a man she barely knew. As a distraction, she asked, "What did you two talk about?"

"When I visited him, he read to me from the thick leather-bound books in his library – novels, philosophy, science. And I in turn, spoke to him of the Magic, and the lore of Mother Ocean. On stormy winter nights we talked about many things, his frustrations with his sister Gormla and the rest of his family – and even of you. In his way your uncle was a worthy guardian of this coast. I will miss him."

He would miss him. "Oh, why did you have to say that? I miss him so much, too. How could I ever have stayed away. And now he's gone, never knowing how much I loved him."

Mara couldn't hold back the flood of her grief any longer. Resting her head against his chest she cried uncontrollably. "There, there, mo chroigh. He knew you loved him – he always knew – no matter how far you journeyed. When hearts and souls speak to one another, words aren't necessary. That's why he wanted you to come back to your real home. He hoped you would claim your true legacy – and me."

Still sobbing and oblivious to their surroundings, she didn't resist when Ronfear guided her to a place where they could sit in the grass out of the wind.

Thoroughly mortified, she tried but couldn't stop the flow of her grief. Never impatient with her for her outburst, Ronfear simply held her. His lips brushed her hair, his voice whispered comforting words in a language that might have been Irish, next to her ear. Spent at last, she sat up and fumbled in her pocket for a crumpled tissue.

"Jesus, Mary and Joseph, I must look a sight, but I do feel better. I didn't cry like this even at the wake."

"Why ever did you deny yourself such a healing? It is a natural and healthy thing to grieve for someone beloved."

Mara didn't answer at first, busying herself with wiping her face and combing her fingers through her hair trying to improve her appearance. Uncomfortable, knowing he was still watching her, she said at last, "Too proud maybe. I didn't fancy breaking down in front of all those people I barely remembered."

Ronfear said nothing, continuing to stare. Growing more agitated under his scrutiny, she at last admitted, "Adam, my fiancé, wouldn't have liked it. He's uncomfortable with Irish displays of emotion. I didn't want to embarrass him." *Or suffer his knife-edged sarcasm.*

"Ah, embarrass him. 'I've never been able to ken the foreigners that come to Eire from across the Mother Ocean. What a warm understanding heart is yours to have such patience with all their strange notions."

Mara flushed. "I'm hardly such a saint as you make me out to be. And I don't think I understand anybody, least of all myself."

"But you are both warm of heart and bright of spirit. I can see it mirrored in the aura-fire that surrounds you. And as to your kenning, I think you understand more than you are allowing yourself to believe. Is that not so?"

"I'm not sure what you mean." Mara's flush deepened and she looked away, searching for the path back to the village. "I have to get back now –"

She hadn't been paying much attention when he brought her to this sheltered place, but as she recognized the place the islanders called, "The Fairy's Pool" her eyes widened.

On Inis Gheal the pool was no grand body of water, only a tiny pond, its jade-green liquid sheltered among great moss covered boulders. Coarse grass covered the slopes of the hollow, while cress and horsetail ferns clustered near the water's edge. To one side of the pool the vegetation had been cut back to reveal long, flat stones buried in the mud. Upon the stones rested a weathered wooden cup and bowl. Next to them, someone had laid an offering of flowers and bread.

A feeling of unreality, sent chills down her backbone. Shrugging out of Ronfear's arms, she rose to her feet. Sensing her change in mood, he asked, "What's wrong?"

Mara hugged herself and refused to look at him. She took a deep breath, but the tremor in her voice she was sure betrayed her nervousness. "N-nothing... I remember this place – that's all. Some of the children took me here once. They swore that if the fairy who lived in its water liked you, your wishes would come true. They said it was a magic place."

Ronfear rose to stand beside her, his eyes suddenly veiled in shadow. "Mara, you look so pale. What's wrong, mo chara?"

"Wrong?" She laughed, feeling on the knife's edge of hysterics. "If I'm remembering correctly – and I believe I am, the Fairy's Pool isn't anywhere near the rocky headland where we were standing before I began blubbering like a baby." Eyes wide, she backed away from him, breathing heavily. "So, how did we come all the way to this pool without me knowing? It's impossible – too far – how did we get here?"

Ronfear shrugged and the pendant about his neck flashed with the movement. Holding out his hands in a placating gesture, he said, "How shall I explain in a way that will not upset you further? Please calm yourself, my dear."

Forcing the words out through trembling lips, Mara said, "Tell me the truth."

"Ah, the truth is it you be wanting, hmm. Shall I tell you that it was my selkie magic that floated us upon the wind to this sacred place? Or, shall I tell you that I guided you while you were so caught up in your mourning that you lost all track of distance and time? Both explanations are true – in their way – I assure you."

Mara let out a frustrated sob and turned her back on him. He was teasing her again. She would like to stomp off in a huff and leave him with his mouth hanging open, but, she couldn't. Why? Because she didn't know the way back to the settlement, damn him, that's why.

"I'm cold and I want to go back to Gran's." Mara hugged herself a little tighter, still shivering. The sun had gone behind a cloudbank, casting violet shadows in the hollow. Stupid, stupid, she was stranded in the middle of nowhere with a crazy man.

Well, Mara, when you go adventuring, you do it in style.

"What did you see when you looked into the pool?" Ronfear asked, changing the subject.

"Huh? Oh, I can't remember. But it must have frightened me. I recall crying all the way back to the village, and only stopped when Gran gave me soda bread with strawberry jam."

Ronfear came up behind her, but didn't touch her this time. His voice was soft, melodic when he finally spoke. "There is an Undine who lives in the pool. This is a sacred place of healing, where anyone of good intent can come and ask for guidance and a blessing. Would you like to look into its waters with me now? You can fill the cup," he pointed to the wooden cup upon the rock, "and drink. Its healing water may ease your heart and help you to understand what is expected of you. Will you do that for me, my heart?" Mara stared at the water, wanting to yield to his suggestion. She took a step toward the spring... Then she flinched as if someone had struck her.

Mara, no!

Mara blinked, suddenly confused. She could have sworn she'd heard her mother's voice. But when she glanced up there was only a gull circling overhead. It screeched again then flew away. Still searching the sky, she fingered her mother's medallion about her neck. It felt heavy and cold. This place was really giving her the creeps.

I should have let Adam handle this. Mama is right. I need to get back to Boston, before I lose all my marbles.

Turning to Ronfear, she shook her head. "No. not now."

"What's that around your neck?"

Startled by the change of topic, she held out the medal to show him. "Nothing really. Just a gift from my mother." Then unwilling to be distracted any longer, she said, "It's getting late. I need to get back. Sean will be coming for me soon."

He seemed disappointed, but after a short hesitation he nodded his agreement. "All right. Perhaps another time." Taking her arm, he led her out of the hollow and back to the well-worn trail that criss-crossed the island.

Coming over a small rise, a group of children saw them, shouted and hurried towards them. Within moments the children were all about them, laughing and babbling in a mixture of English and Irish. One little tyke held out her arms and Ronfear lifted her onto his shoulder.

His brown eyes solemn, a sturdy lad of about five or six with a tangled thatch of dark hair, blocked the trail directly in front of them. "Athair, Gran says that the boat is coming across for the lady; Mr. MacCarthaigh will be here soon."

Ronfear made a motion for the boy to proceed them and they started walking again. "Lead on, mo mhic, show us the way."

Mara watched the children running and playing around them with a deep longing. Unlike her earlier meeting with them, in Ronfear's presence they weren't quiet or shy. "I believe that boy called you athair. That's Gaelic for father isn't it?"

Ronfear smiled and tickled the tot on his shoulder, making her laugh. "Yes, he is my son Rory and this is my beautiful big girl Ethne."

"She is lovely. I'm looking forward to having children of my own once Adam and I are married. How many children do you have?"

"On Inis Gheal, only my little beauty here and the rascal you mentioned."

Mara raised an eyebrow, then just to tease him, she asked, "On Inis Gheal, eh? And how many children do you have elsewhere?"

Ronfear shrugged. "How many? I don't know. But I have only these two human children at the moment."

Mara flushed and looked away, once more aware of his strangeness. Had she really expected a sane answer from a man who was delusional? Holy Mother Mary, how much farther was it to the village? She needed to get away from the guy.

Masking her unease with sarcasm she continued to joke, "Only two human children. And being a selkie I suppose all the rest are seals, right?"

Ronfear flashed her his winning smile and nodded.

Ah, there was the first of the cottages. "Oh, please. Give me a break." Tired of humoring him, Mara angrily pushed past him to follow the children back to the village.

Ronfear stared at her retreating back, openmouthed. "What did I do? Women, will I ever understand them?"

USING A BOUT OF PLAY with his daughter as an excuse, Ronfear deliberately lagged behind Mara and the children, allowing Rory to take over as her escort.

Did the woman know what she was wearing? Sly as the witch that bore her, was she taunting him with her power? No, he didn't think so. But the charm she wore had certainly set his plans awry this day. Mara herself was far more complex than the women to whom he'd grown accustomed. She both frightened and intrigued him. He needed more time to study and woo her – but did they have such a luxury as time?

She could leave for America any day, and that would be a disaster for them all. Their fate lay in his hands; he dared not fail. The Elder would be furious if he learned of Ronfear's botched effort to win her compliance today. It would be a heavy blow to his pride, but perhaps he should go to his father and ask for his help, before the Elder scried out the truth and came seeking him.

Still keeping his distance, Ronfear watched Mara and the children arrive at Gran's cottage. Trailing the old woman, MacCarthy came out a moment later. Ronfear ducked behind the corner of Turlouch's cottage until Mara and Gran had said their farewells, and she had followed the Northern Man down the trail to the beach.

When he risked another peek, they were gone, but Gran was still there talking earnestly to his son. Fearing more women trouble if she saw him, he ducked back behind the wall. At last he heard Gran's door slam and risked another look. Only Rory remained outside, glancing round as if searching for someone.

Spotting his father at last, he hurried over to him. "Athair, Gran wants to talk to you."

Why was he not surprised. "Mm, does she now." He jiggled Ethne, making her giggle. "Well, you're a good boy to tell me. I'll come in a while."

Rory looked at him sternly, folding his thin arms across his chest in imitation of his grandma. "She will be cross with you if you don't come now."

Ronfear smiled, ruffled his son's hair and gave him a wink."She will be cross with me only if you tell her that you found me."

When Rory looked worried by his suggestion, Ronfear proposed a distraction. "I will go talk to Gran, to be sure, but first let's go walk along the beach and maybe go for a swim. You would like that, I think, hmm?"

"Oh yes, I would like that very much." Rory smiled, becoming excited. "Will the Elder join us? Can we go now?"

The Elder. ...Ronfear's stomach lurched; just whom he didn't want to see any time soon. Then he laughed at his foolish worries. All wasn't lost, to be sure. Only half listening to Rory telling him about going fishing with Turlouch, Ronfear accompanied the children to the beach.

DURING HER RIDE BACK to the manor, Mara sternly told herself to "get a grip" and stop being foolish. Though she found him disturbingly attractive, Ronfear was nothing more than a poor deluded crazy man who had tricked her some how. Nothing magical had happened to her – nothing. Only children believed in such nonsense. She would let Adam handle her business affairs from now on.

Determined to forget about Ronfear and her disconcerting visit to the island, Mara ignored Una's anxious looks, Adam's sly hints to come home, and the maddening phone calls from her mother. Instead she spent the next couple of days plunged wholeheartedly into the mountain of work needing her attention around the manor.

On the morning of the third day after her visit to Inis Gheal she was awakened out of restless sleep by the barking of seals in the cove below her window. At first the sound seemed a continuation of her dreams. Then, more awake, Mara groaned. She had the odd notion that the seals were calling to her, wanting her to come down to them, but she resisted such a bizarre notion. It was far too early to consider getting up for a walk on the beach. It was barely light out there, the grey mists still shrouding the bay.

She was just settling back when the ringing telephone jarred her awake again.

"Hello? Oh, hi, Mama," Mara yawned and glanced at the clock beside the bed. "Jeez, Mama, it's four in the morning. What are you doing awake so late? Isn't it after midnight over there? Is something wrong?"

"Oh, my girl, sorry if I woke you, but I have to talk to you, ask you a question."

Mara yawned again. "A question? Couldn't it have waited till later – when I'm more awake and had my tea?"

"Listen to me, Mara; this is important. I've seen him – in my dreams again – and I'm afraid for you. Please my girl, promise me you will come home."

Promises. Hadn't someone else recently been talking about promises needing to be remembered and kept? Hmmm...

"Mara, my baby, my dear child, are you there? Are you still wearing my gift? Are you listening to me?"

"Yes, Mama, I'm here – I'm wearing the medal and listening, but you're not making much sense." Mara could picture her mother's heart-shaped face unnaturally pale, her green eyes clouded by anxiety, her hands trembling as she gripped the phone. Her mother usually denied having any trace of what the old Irish called, "The Sight." For her to mention her dreams meant she was truly worried. Fully awake, Mara's stomach gave an uneasy flutter.

There was a long pause, finally Gormla said, "I'm trying. There's this man, you see, some might think him handsome, but he's a devil really, and you being so innocent and all – I had to warn you!"

Innocent, her? She was pushing thirty and had been sexually active since her last year of high school. "Mama, please. Just ask your question so I can get back to sleep."

"Don't rush me, you sassy child, this isn't easy for me."

No, it probably wasn't, if sex was involved. Raised in a catholic boarding school, Gormla found even the thought of sex distressing. Or so her father claimed, when he'd been too drunk to mind who heard him.

Sitting up in bed, she adjusted her pillows, and temporized, "Sorry, Mama, I can tell by your voice that this is important to you. I'm awake – and listening. Ask me anything you want."

Gormla took a deep breath and began, as usual, in the most roundabout fashion. "Mara dear, when I returned home after the troubles there was this man – he tried to – he spoke of love and partnership, but all he really wanted was to ruin me. An honest marriage consecrated in Holy Church was never part of his evil scheme. And when I wouldn't submit to his insulting proposition he tried to force me. But I was too strong for all his conjuring and that of his black-hearted kin.

"I left Ireland soon after that and no amount of pleading by my mother could weaken my resolve to return. For the sake of my immortal soul and those of my future children, I gladly gave up my inheritance. In America I thought you would be safe, but I was wrong. My own treacherous brother and those soulless devils worked their evil spells and I failed to recognize your danger in time."

Mara listened, fascinated. She doubted if Gormla had ever told anyone this story before. So much of her mother's eccentric behavior now made sense. Cursed by her Catholic education, as well as growing up before Women's Lib and the freedom of Mara's own generation, she suddenly felt sorry for her.

"I appreciate you sharing this with me, Mama, but I still don't understand what all that has to do with me being here in Ireland now?"

"I told you all this, because Ronfear, according to my dream, is still living on or near Inis Gheal. And if you let him, he will have his way with you, and damn your immortal soul forever."

Ronfear? Surely it couldn't be the same man. Her mother was old – and Ronfear was – hadn't he said that he and Uncle Seamas used to talk about Gormla? But surely if he'd actually known her mother, he'd met her when he was just a wee lad – surely.

"Mara, are you still there?"

"Yes, Mama, I'm still here."

"Well, have you met him, or any dark- haired man who talks to you of love and has tried to have his way with you? Have you?"

Not willing to admit to anything, until she'd had time to think, Mara hedged, "No, Mama, I haven't been seduced by any such man. So, stop worrying and go to bed. Adam is coming back any day now, and we both will be home soon."

After hanging up the phone, Mara found she was too restless to sleep. Maybe she should get back. Her classes would be starting in less than a month. One more day should clear up most of the important things needing to be tackled around the manor. And if she met with the solicitor tomorrow...

Of course that still wouldn't solve the larger issue, whether to sell the islands. No matter. Mara could use some of her personal savings to pay Sean and Una and the worst of the debts in the meantime.

Dressing in warm clothes and rubber boots, she tiptoed out of the house and headed for the beach. She could still hear the seals barking, somewhere out in the fog. She hated to admit it—even to herself, but her mother's call had upset her. Maybe a walk along the shore would do her some good and settle her chaotic mind.

Wearing nothing but his shell pendant and a pair of raggedy cut-off jeans, Ronfear was waiting for her near the base of the cliff. He smiled when he saw her, hair sleeked back and dripping. Maybe she should have been, but Mara wasn't surprised to see him. "Aren't you cold?"

"No, I'm used to the Irish weather."

"Mm, you must be to swim on a day like this. I shiver just thinking about it."

"Come for a walk with me then. If I can't interest you in an early morning swim, maybe a walk along the beach will warm your thin Yankee blood." Ronfear held out his hand to her and after a moment of hesitation, she took it.

The tide was out, the morning air cool upon her face. Beads of moisture clung to her wavy auburn hair and her fleece jacket. In the distance a foghorn moaned. Nearby gulls argued over debris washed up upon the shore. They headed away from the boathouse, toward a rocky point that she could just make out through the shifting mist.

"The sea, the mist, the waves crashing against the shore, it's so beautiful. My father used to tease me that I must have webbed feet like a duck, to always enjoy the fog and the rain."

Ronfear cocked his head to one side, eyeing her. "I don't understand. Webbed feet, like a duck? Or do you mean a seal maybe? Not many ducks round here"

Mara laughed. "Never mind; it's just a silly saying we have in America."

"Oh. But perhaps your affinity for the magic is found in the element of Water," Ronfear suggested. "As is mine."

Mara made a noncommittal noise, only half-listening to what he was saying. She definitely needed to talk to him about her mother's phone call, but she'd also wanted to wait till she'd had time to sort things out in her own mind first. And yet, the longer she kept silent, the harder it was going to be to broach the subject with him. So maybe it was a good thing he'd shown up so unexpectedly this morning. But how to begin without looking like an utter fool?

She was still debating how to broach the subject with him as they rounded the point. Ronfear led her into a sheltered hollow among the rocks and sat her down on a bed of dried seaweed and debris. "You are shaking with the morning chill, my heart. Do you want to return to the manor?"

"No. I'll be all right, and I need to talk to you."

Touching his lips to her forehead in a brief kiss, he disappeared among the rocks closer to the water, then returned a moment later with a dark bundle under one arm. Crouching beside her, Ronfear shook out the bundle and wrapped it about her shoulders. "Is that better?" he asked and sat down next to her.

The bundle was some kind of cloak or blanket, covered with a sleek, but coarse gray fur. It also reeked of fish. She wrinkled up her nose, and he laughed. "What is this?"

Eyes alight with amusement, he put an arm about her shoulder, leaned over and kissed her, this time upon the lips. "Why, it's my sealskin, of course."

The kiss was soft, fleeting, a mere brushing of his lips across hers. But Mara felt her bones melting at his touch. *Get a grip, Mara, don't let yourself get distracted by his nearness.*

Mara shifted, putting a bit of distance between them. "Mm, right. You're a selkie, I forgot. OK, I'll play along with your game. If this is indeed your sealskin, aren't you afraid I might steal it away from you and hide it? According to the old legends, that's the time-honored way for a mortal to capture a selkie."

Pulling aside a corner of the furry blanket, he slipped under it with her, and cradled her against his chest. He kissed her again, longer and deeper this time. "So the legends say, true enough." His hand slid under her jacket, coming to rest against the bare skin of her breasts. He kissed her once more, his eyes luminous with awakened desire. "Have you considered that I might *want* you to capture me, mo chroigh?"

Oh, merciful heaven, Mara felt as if she were drowning in a sea of desire. She liked what his tongue and his warm expressive hands were doing to her – how he was making her body feel.

Of a sudden Ronfear let out a startled grunt of pain and jerked his hand away from her neck. At almost the same moment, Mara heard her mother's voice as clear as if she were standing just behind them.

Mara stop! If you let him have his way with you he will damn your immortal soul.

Mara felt goosebumps crawling across her skin. What was happening to her? Hearing voices, was she becoming as daft as her parent? She didn't believe for a moment that sex before marriage would damn her soul, yet as she recalled her mother's phone call, she couldn't banish the feeling of danger from her mind.

But how could this warm and vital, though enigmatic man, lying beside her be the same man who had tried to seduce her mother more than forty years before? It just wasn't possible – it wasn't. no one could look that good and be that old.

Confused and slightly ill, she took a ragged breath, and gently, but firmly pushed him away. Then she sat up and pulled down her clothes. Why was she letting this happen to her? She and Adam had been having their troubles, but having an affair with someone she barely knew, when her wedding date was already booked – well, it wasn't right.

"Please, don't do this to me, Ronfear, please."

His voice a lilting murmur, he asked, "What is it, mo chroigh? Did I hurt you? Don't you like what I am doing?"

Mara choked on a laugh that was almost a sob and pulled the hood of her jacket over her head, so he couldn't see the expression on her face. "Maybe I like what we are doing too well. That's the problem."

He rose up on an elbow, trying to see her better. "Problem? How is that a problem?"

"It just is, damn it."

"Oh." His brow wrinkled in thought, he sat up. "Don't push me away, my heart. We are meant to be together. You will never have what you truly want, or be at peace, if you wed a foreigner in far America."

Trembling, her eyes stinging, she hugged herself and shifted away from him even farther. "I don't know what you're talking about."

He barked a laugh. "You don't? This wild coastland cries out to your soul. In Americay you are a shadow woman living a lie. Seamas knew that. He promised – he wanted us to be together. Your roots are here, your heart is here and, and I need you."

Startled, she turned round to stare. He sighed and nodded. "Yes, mo chroigh, it's true. I can't protect the coast and the islands by myself. There is so much about your modern world I don't understand. I need your help."

Was he working for Greenpeace or some Irish environmental organization? That would explain a lot if true. Should she be flattered or insulted by his attempted seduction? Mara chuckled and relaxed. "You don't need me – not really. The wild life sanctuary uncle founded won't be affected if I sell Inis Gheal or keep it. Let your mind be easy about that."

Ronfear stared at her as if she had just sprouted horns. Finally he took a deep breath, and in a quiet voice, he said, "Please stay and let me love you. Don't let what your family has worked so hard to protect for centuries be destroyed by the money-men who don't understand us."

Ronfear's musky animal allure was almost overpowering. Mara's body ached for his caress and the idyllic life he offered. But the rational part of her mind warned, that she couldn't just abandon her fiancé, her job, and her life in Boston. How would they live if she did?

Choking on a sob, she shook her head. "I can't. Ronfear, it wouldn't solve the problem if I did stay. What you're saying—it's just a fairytale; the world doesn't work like that. I know Uncle Seamas wanted me to carry on here. But all that takes money – money I don't have. I hate the idea of selling the island like Adam wants, but I don't see another solution. I wish I did."

As she continued to speak, her words kindled a spark of anger in the depths of his eyes. His accent thickened, and his voice, managed to blend both pity and bitterness when he replied "Fairytales is it, that I'm a-speaking? Ah, Mara, has your barren life across the water robbed you of your faith in the Isles' magic? Too bad you have forgotten. Perhaps The Burke was wrong about you. Maybe there is more of your mother in you than he chose to believe."

Mara felt the flush heating her face as her own temper ignited. "My mother. Yes, let's talk about *my mother.* She called me this morning – did the selkie magic you claim to have tell you?"

Ronfear hesitated, his eyes hooded, suddenly wary. "No. I didn't know. I'd forgotten that now human technology has magic of its own to rival that of even the most powerful among the Sidhe. What did she say to you? Anything about me?"

Clutching the saint's medallion, Mara gave a brittle laugh. "Oh yes, quite a lot actually. She said she'd seen you in her dreams. She warned me to stay away from you. She has some pretty wild notions—including that you tried to seduce her once. Or at least some man calling himself Ronfear did. So, did you or one of your relatives do that?"

"Did I do what?"

Mara made a disgusted growl deep in her throat. "Don't *you* play games with *me*," she snapped. "You know what I'm asking."

He sighed, not meeting her eye. "Yes, maybe I do." Ronfear cupped sand and debris in his palm, allowing it to slip through his hand in a steady brown ribbon. Mara waited, glaring. At last his palm was empty. He took a deep breath and looked into her eyes. "I believe, as I think you do as well, that Gormla is a very bitter and troubled woman. Your Uncle spoke of her many times, sometimes with affection, sometimes with anger, and always with regret."

"But did you know her personally?"

"I am older than you assume, mo chroigh. Yes, I knew her; she was a beautiful young woman. But she was so afraid – of me, of everything." His eyes pleading he held out his hands to her. "I was so ignorant, and my father was too impatient – but you are not your mother. In the short time I have known you, I have grown to respect you, and maybe love you – in the way of my kind. For us it would be different. I promise."

"How old are you?" He shrugged.

Sometimes she wondered how to take the guy—was he serious? Was he that out of touch with reality? Mara took a deep breath. "Okay, did you try to seduce her as she claims? Oh god, why am I asking such a stupid question? I must be going out of my mind!"

"I don't know what she claims, my heart. All I know is that she misunderstood what was offered, and chose to break with your family's tradition."

"Family tradition. A tradition I've never heard of." This strange conversation was giving her a headache. She needed to get back to the manor, if she planned to get any work done that day. Crazy, the man was certifiably crazy. There was no such thing as magic; why was she listening to any of his nonsense?

Oh how she suddenly longed for the safety and sanity of her own home in Boston. Not able to meet his eye, Mara rose and started down the beach. "I have to get back. Sean and Una will be wondering where I've gone."

Growling something unintelligible under his breath, he draped his seal skin over one shoulder and went after her. As he caught up, he snapped, "So, is your mind made up then? Will you do as the money man wants and sell the Bright Island?"

Mara spun round, glaring, a flush heating her cheeks. "No. My mind's not made up. You and the people here are pulling me one way, my mother and Adam another. I'm caught in the middle, and damn it, it's tearing me apart. Can't all of you see that and leave me alone."

"All right." Ronfear folded his arms across his chest, returning the glare. "If I can't convince you to stay with me in Ireland then make my daughter your heir and I will buy the islands from you."

"What? Buy Inis Gheal? How could you do that?"

Ronfear barked a bitter laugh. "There is gold in the sea, woman. If you force me to, I will obtain what is necessary and pay your price."

"But if you knew where there was sunken treasure or some such, why didn't you give it to my Uncle before this?"

"Because he wouldn't accept it."

"But why ever not? It would have solved so many of his problems."

"It might have solved some but created others. Think, Mara, what would happen to the seal isles and my beautiful wild ocean if word got out that treasure could be found hereabouts?"

He did have a point there; she could understand both Ronfear's and her uncle's reluctance not to let that be known, no matter how desperate their circumstances.

"I *can* understand how you might perceive your situation as being like a fish struggling in a net, not of your own making," he added in a softer voice. "But consider well. For you will have to live with the consequences of what you decide."

Was he threatening her? She wasn't sure, his expression was solemn, but not menacing. Yet some deeply buried instinct warned her of the truth in his words. "I need to get back." A slight nod and he took her hand and they continued down the beach.

When they came near the trail leading up to the house, Mara saw Sean MacCarthaigh striding purposefully towards them. As he recognized Ronfear, his face darkened. Too late, she realized she was still holding Ronfear's hand and removed it, stepping away.

Sean gave her a sour look, then focused his ire on Ronfear. "I thought I told you not to come back round here. This is private property; we've no use for a lazy, no-acount rascal with tinker ways. So, clear off, boyo."

Ronfear's jaw tightened, but he held his ground. "Private property, is it now. And would you be speaking of the beach, MacCarthaigh, or the woman?"

Sean's face turned a dangerous shade of purple. "Both, ya' bacachd. Get the hell out of here, before I call the gardai and have you arrested."

Eyes suddenly as hard as daggers, Ronfear gave Sean a feral smile that emphasized the elongated points of his canines. "Have a care how you speak to me, northern man. The beach belongs to the seals and the ocean. Remember that when next you take your boat to Inis Gheal. And as for you protecting her for the absent boyfriend," Ronfear's smile widened. "If he values what he thinks he has, then let him come and claim her."

"OK, that does it; this macho posturing has gone on long enough," Mara cried. "You pair of idiots, I'm not a piece of 'property' to be fought over, damn it, so just back off, both of you. Mr. MacCarthaigh, I don't need you playing guard dog; I'm not a child."

Sean's glare was murderous, but he bobbed his head in acquiescence.

Next Mara rounded on Ronfear. "I think you should go now. Like you said, I have to make my own choice. I will let you know what I decide."

"So be it then. I'll be near if you want me – you need only call and I'll come." Then, without a backward glance, he headed into the fog. Mara watched him till he vanished in the mist. Then she turned and started up the cliff, a sullen MacCarthaigh trailing in her wake.

SEAN KEPT OUT OF MARA'S way for the rest of the day, but his disapproval was a brooding presence in the house, even when he went to town on an errand of his own. The weather was miserable, the mist turning to rain. Mara retired to the library and tried to focus on her course outlines for a change, but working on her schoolwork only made her homesick for Adam and her cozy study in Boston. Picking up the phone, she dialed Adam's office, but she'd forgotten about the time difference and he was out. She hung up, her eyes stinging.

Oh what should she do? She was dabbing at her eyes with a tissue, when she became aware of someone watching her. Una was standing in the doorway. "I came to tell you that dinner will be ready soon, will you be wanting to eat with me and Sean in the kitchen? Or would you like a tray brought in here?"

Mara wasn't hungry, but supposed she should eat. Suffering through a meal with Sean giving her his black looks, was the last thing she needed at that moment, however. "I'll take a tray in here. I have to get some work for the university done."

Una turned to leave, hesitated, then came further into the room instead. Glancing anxiously over her shoulder, Una took a deep breath and said in a voice barely above a whisper, "About the property, Miss Mara, Sean didn't want me to tell you because he's got his back up after this morning. He's a good man in his way but, him coming from Belfast during the Troubles and all, he doesn't understand about Inis Gheal. I thought you ought to know that last spring there was a man name of O'Shea and his wife come by to talk to Mr. Burke. They weren't interested in the islands, only the manor. They wanted to make it into a hotel, you see."

Mara sat up a little straighter; Una had her full attention now. "What did Uncle Seamas think of the idea?"

"Mr. Burke was polite to them, but he didn't want to sell. All the same Mr. O'Shea gave him his card before he left. If you could talk to him..." Una studied Mara's face, her eyes pleading, but there was a stubborn set to her jaw, and Mara recognized the implied challenge. "Since you say you don't want to sell the Bright Isle –" She broke off at Sean's shout from the kitchen. "I got to go. I'll bring your tray up shortly."

When she was gone, Mara leaned back in her chair and considered. If the O'Shea's were still interested, that would certainly solve the problem for the people on Inis Gheal. But what about her? She wanted to help, but did she want to help the islanders that much? Mara couldn't imagine spending her summers renting a room in a hotel that had once been her uncle's home. Then her own words to Ronfear returned to haunt her.

Mara, what a hypocrite you are.

She stewed about the problem all during her solitary meal. Then, seeing Una's hopeful face as she cleared away the tray, Mara decided that she owed it to the islanders to, at least talk to this Mr. O'Shea – if she could locate him – and she told Una so.

Seamas must have thrown Mr. O'Shea's card away, but when Adam called just before bed, she broached the subject with him. There was a long silence on the other end of the line, finally growing impatient, she snapped, "Well, is it feasible for us to do it?"

"Making the manor into a hotel, at least in theory, has possibilities. But I can't imagine anyone considering it seriously. There is so much work that would have to be done on the place, and it would take a lot of ready capital to make the venture profitable. But – Mara, why on earth would you want to sell the house? I thought that was where your memories are, not on some barren island stuck out in the middle of nowhere."

"I do have pleasant memories about being here, but I have to consider more than just my memories. The islanders –"

"Maybe your mother has a point about how the place affects people. You aren't being rational about this. You've told me yourself that for much of the winter Inis Gheal is totally cut off from the rest of Ireland by storms. And even the summer weather is unpredictable. Do you want to sell your family's ancestral home and move into some fisherman's shack?"

Becoming impatient with him, she snapped, "Adam, I don't want to argue with you over this. All I want is your business opinion, and how best to go about finding this O'Shea fellow. That's all."

Becoming cross in turn, he shot back, "All right, damn it. I'll ask Laurence to contact his realtor friend tomorrow. I'll let you know what he says. Will that satisfy you?"

"Yes."

That night Mara's sleep was more troubled than usual. In the dream she wandered the rocky hillsides of Inis Gheal, searching for something that always eluded her. Finally heartsick and discouraged, she allowed herself to be guided by instinct to the one place she'd been avoiding, The Fairy's Pool.

It was twilight in her dream vision of the sheltered cove, violet shadows, clinging to the sentinel rocks that guarded the indigo pool. Silver moonlight glinted off the ripples made by the water welling up from the spring deep within the island's core. No sound but the water's murmur broke the stillness.

Then Mara saw a man kneeling by the altar stone at the edge of the pool. At first he was only a dark silhouette to her dream sight, but as she focused her eye upon him, she knew him. It was Uncle Seamas. Mara crossed to the edge of the pool and sank to her knees beside him. The ghost turned his head and smiled at her.

"Hello, my girl, I've been waiting for you."

"Oh, uncle, I'm so confused. I don't know what to do. Why did you leave me with so many hard choices?"

Seamas waved his hand to encompass the pool and the land beyond. "The love of this land is the well spring that nourishes your soul, Mara. Is claiming your inheritance such a hard thing for you, or only for your mother?"

Her first impulse was to hotly deny his accusation, but ensnared by his otherworldly stare, the words wouldn't come. At last she said, "It shames me to acknowledge it, but I could have come back to Ireland like you wanted, uncle. Like I wanted. It was always mama who didn't want me to come. And no matter how hard I try to fight her, I always cave into her wishes in the end."

The ghost nodded his sympathy. "Gormla is a strong woman, to be sure. But so are you, my dear. Now that you are a woman grown, isn't it time you take charge of your own life?

"But I *have* taken charge of my life. I'm my own person. I have my degree and a good job. That's a lot for a poor Irish emigrant to achieve. I also have a fiancé who has a bright future and will be a good provider for me and our children. I am the envy of every single woman in Boston. And mama has nothing to do with any of that."

Ignoring her flare of temper, the ghost answered in a calm voice. "They are great accomplishments for anyone, to be sure, if they are your heart's desire. Otherwise they are meaningless victories in an unhappy life. Are you happy, my girl?"

Mara opened her mouth to say yes, then hesitated. She couldn't lie to him, not in this sacred place. Nor could she lie to herself. "I don't know. Until I returned to Ireland I thought so. But once I am married I will be happy, I'm certain of it. Adam and the life we will have together will be a dream come true."

"A dream come true. Ah, but is the dream yours, my girl, or your mother's?" Seamas chuckled when he saw her startled expression. "Adam is the man you have sought and won, but I doubt if he is a kindred spirit to your own. No, I think he is the man your *mother* thought would be a good match and future provider."

The ghost laid a comforting hand on her shoulder. "Don't look so surprised. I've watched your man reading my legal papers, exploring my house and land, seeing how much money there is to be made. Cold, logical Adam isn't the choice of your heart, Mara, but Gormla's. My sister would have been willing to sell her soul to the very devil if that would have won her a man like Adam Bensen, instead of the hard-working, hard-drinking Irishman she settled for."

"...I believe there is some truth in what you have told me, Uncle Seamas, but I will have to think about it some more before I cancel my wedding plans."

"You do that, my girl. You are a strong woman. I have faith in you. Now that your eyes are opened to the truth you will do what is best for all of us. I am sure of it."

"Uncle, I wish I had as much confidence in me as you do. I feel so confused, like I've made a mess of everything. Please, tell me what to do?"

The ghost shook his head and got to his feet. "I'm not my sister. I cannot do that. You must choose for yourself, Mara."

But Mara seemed so forlorn, the ghost offered her one more piece of advice, before he faded away. "The Fairy's Pool is a sacred place, a healing place. Make an offering, drink of its water and perhaps you will find what you seek."

A place of healing. ... After a moment's hesitation, Mara filled the cup and drank.

The liquid was sweet and cool. Then, looking down upon the altar, she saw as if through a transparency, the image of the gift that had lain upon the stone in the daytime world. An offering. She must make an offering if she wanted guidance. Her spirit-eye glanced about the hollow, searching. She had no bread, no flowers and no idea what else would be appropriate.

What could she give that was hers alone – and valuable? Mara thought about it for a while, but she had brought nothing of value into the dream, except the necklace she constantly wore around her neck. Mama would be cross with her if she gave it away, but her need for advice was too important to worry about that now. The chain was made of gold; she would offer it to the fairy in exchange for her help. The clasp wouldn't open, so Mara lifted it over her head instead. As she did a few auburn hairs tangled in its chain. Looping the chain over a plant growing beside the pool, she allowed the rest to trail down into the indigo water.

"Lady, this is all new to me. I hope this gift is appropriate. I need your guidance."

Still on her knees with head bowed as if in prayer, Mara at first didn't see the spirit she'd summoned. Then, becoming aware of a light, Mara looked up. Bathed in a silver radiance, the vision before her had a woman's shape from the waist up, and the body and fan-like tail of a fish below. Her hair was long and pale, falling forward to cover her small breasts. Her features were comely in the human fashion, but her skin glinted with minute silver scales when she moved. When she met Mara's eye she smiled.

"Welcome, I have been waiting such a long time to greet you, did you know? Your magical gift makes us sisters of a sort."

"Sisters?" Mara was puzzled. "I have no gills."

The Undine's laugh was as merry as a mountain stream flowing over the smooth pebbles of its bed. "No gills, but your affinity for the element of Water will allow you to summon its elemental magic for a time, should you ever need it."

"I still don't think I understand."

"No matter; you will when the time is right. It was very clever of you to come to me in your dream, very clever indeed and none too soon."

"I don't feel very clever at all. I've no idea what I did to get here."

The Fairy's smile was enigmatic. Mara decided not to waste time on unnecessary questions, now that she had summoned the guardian by whatever means. In a flood she poured out the entire tale of her predicament.

The Undine listened without interruption. When Mara finished, she said, "I'm afraid I can't tell you what you should do. The decision is yours, and only yours, to make."

Up to her. "Can't you give me any advice that might help me?"

The Undine let out her silvery laugh again, but her sea-green eyes were stern. "I can't use my magic to make up your mind for you, if that is what you want. You are still a creature of free will." Then, the spirit relented, and offered, "Well, there is one service I can do for you. I will allow you to look into my mirror. If your magic is strong, and you have the courage, you may obtain knowledge that will aid you."

Was she strong enough to see into her future—see what? Did she have another option? No, she didn't. "I will look into your mirror. Thank you."

"So be it, then." Reaching a slender webbed hand into the water, the lady drew up a dripping obsidian hand mirror, tangled about with waterweed. Its surface was dark, not reflecting Mara's face, when the fairy held it up to show her. "Look deep into its center, focus your intent and see what has been kept hidden..."

Mara stared into the mirror, gathering her chaotic thoughts into a question. "Show me what I need to know, so I can choose wisely what I'm to do with uncle's inheritance."

The surface remained dark for a time, then a violet light formed at its center, flowing outward in a widening spiral. When the mirror was bathed totally in the light, another image appeared in its depths.

To her surprise Mara saw her mother. Gormla was dressed, in her favorite green velvet lounging robe, the one that complimented her green eyes and dyed auburn hair. She sat in her comfortable reading chair, phone in hand, a cup of tea on the table beside her. The scene was so familiar that Mara smiled, but there was nothing amusing about the grim expression distorting her mother's pale, heart-shaped face. As she listened, Gormla said, "You're wrong, Adam Bensen. Where Ireland and those islands are concerned, Mara is not a sensible girl."

Gormla listened, her face flushing a deep crimson. "Don't talk to me of your projects. I'm tired of your excuses. Take what MacCarthaigh told you seriously. You bring her home."

When she hung up the phone, Gormla sat very still, her hands clasped tight in her lap, staring straight ahead, her mouth set in a thin hard line. Mara knew that look; she'd seen it many times as a child and had grown to fear it. And as if in confirmation, her mother's next words sent a lance of dread stabbing into her soul.

"She lied to me – me, her own mother! Such a beautiful young girl – I knew she would be lost to me and the Holy Church once her blood began to flow. They would take her then – for him. I thought it was finished when the servant did my bidding and her father died during one of his frequent debauches. With him gone I could keep her safe in Boston with me. but I was wrong. The taint is in her blood, curse them, as it is in mine. I must summon the creature once again."

Gormla rose, and the room was plunged into darkness. Only her mother's chilling words echoed through the blackness as the magic and her dream faded. "I'd rather see her dead and her immortal soul safe, than let them corrupt her with their evil sorcery."

NEXT MORNING MARA AWOKE more exhausted than when she'd gone to bed. She was vaguely aware of discovering something both terrible and important in her dream, but she refused to let it surface and spoil her day. Fleeing her thoughts as if they were wolves, she hurriedly dressed, her mind on coffee and a meal.

As she was pulling the comforter back into place upon the bed, the gleam of something metallic caught her eye. Pulling back the sheet, Mara picked up the medallion that her mother had given her. Her hand flew to her neck, but its golden chain was gone. How had it come off – and where was the chain? Mara searched under the bed and among the sheets, but couldn't find it. Deciding to look for it later she tossed the medallion into a dresser drawer and went down to the kitchen.

Both MacCarthaighs were there, Sean reading the paper, Una doing something at the stove. Mara slid into a chair at the table and Una brought her a cup of coffee. Sean, seemingly still cross with her grunted a greeting, then buried his face in his paper once more. Mara flushed, then looked away. How childish men could be. The sun was streaming through the kitchen window and birds were singing outside. She took a deep breath, letting go of her pique with a long sigh. It was too fine a day to be cross with anyone.

"What do you have planned for today, Miss Mara," Una said as she set a plate of eggs on the table by her elbow. "There are a few more trunks to go through in the attic. Shall we get started on them after I clean up the breakfast dishes?"

Mara considered as she chewed a mouthful of eggs. The thought of more dusty trunks depressed her. Glancing once more outside at the sunshine she shook her head. "Not today, I should go see uncle's solicitor again."

Then seeing Una's disappointment, she proposed, "Una, it's too beautiful outside to be cooped up inside sifting through old dusty heirlooms. After talking to the solicitor, I think I want to relax and play tourist for a change. Why don't you and I go down to Galway. You can be my guide, show me some of the local sights of interest. Would you like that?"

Sean snapped down his paper and glared, but Una ignored his scowling face. "What a grand idea, Miss Mara. You've not seen much of Ireland – not since your childhood, I think. Glad I would be ta' be your guide."

They left mid-morning and Una was enjoying herself so much by evening that Mara suggested they stay over for a day or two in a hotel, before heading back to the manor. Una was reluctant at first, saying Sean might worry, but Mara talked her round.

Truth be told, Mara wasn't having quite so much fun, but she decided Una needed the outing as much, if not more than she did. Sean, the scowling macho bastard, probably never took her anywhere. Her mood almost manic in her determination to forget Ronfear, the manor and all her worries, Mara through herself with a will into the venture and had the satisfaction of knowing she had given Una a wonderful treat.

In late afternoon of the third day, a tired but smiling Una and Mara arrived back at the manor with the back seat of the car loaded down with luggage and parcels. When they pulled up, Sean came out of the kitchen to help unload the car. Una gave him a kiss and apologized for being gone so long.

To Mara's surprise and delight, Adam opened the front door and walked slowly down the steps. Adam enfolded her in his arms and treated her to a long welcoming kiss.

"Mmm, Adam, that was wonderful. What a nice surprise but what are you doing here?"

Adam kissed her hungrily again, but when he spoke at last she detected the faintest note of petulance in his tone of voice. "I got to missing you too much to stay away. But when I get here expecting to receive a warm welcome from my sweetie, I find only a grumpy caretaker and no supper. Sean tells me that you women left that very morning to play the tourists in Galway."

Mara laughed and kissed him. "My poor, poor dear, I'm so sorry, but I did need a break from this dreary place." She took his hand and they walked towards the house. "Mmm, I'm sure I can think of some way to make it up to you. Just wait till I get you upstairs and into my bed and I'll show you how warm and welcoming I can be."

Adam chuckled and gave her a little pat on the ass. "Hmm, I bet you can at that. I can hardly wait. I would hate to have come all this way for nothing."

AFTER ADAM AND MARA disappeared into the house talking happily among themselves. Sean muttered a curse under his breath and grabbed some of the luggage from the car. "Arrogant foreigner, he could have helped."

When Una hurried to help him, he waved her away and motioned with his head to the garden. "Don't trouble yourself. I'll get them. You have visitors."

"Visitors?" With a bag still in her hand, she turned in the direction he pointed. Turlouch and her sister were standing concealed in the shadows. Una's face blanched. "What's happened – did they say? Is it Ma?"

Sean muttered another curse. He glanced at the two Islanders, then returned his glare to Una. "Since when do your relatives tell me aught of importance?"

"But for them to be here at such a time means trouble –"

"– Then ask them yourself, if you've a mind. I'm but the Northern Man. Not good enough for the like o' them."

Fear igniting her temper, she snapped, "I will, then." Dropping the bag on the ground, Una hurried over to them.

"May all the saints and the Good People protect us, you've finally come back," her sister said. "The black-hearted witch has betrayed us, curse her soul!"

Black-hearted witch? Had Gormla Burke returned? A shiver running down her backbone, Una glanced at the house, but Sean and the others were inside and out of earshot. "Keep your voice down, foolish woman. Come inside. I'll fix us a cup of tea and you can tell me what's wrong."

"I'll not go in – not with that treacherous woman in there." Her sister glared with loathing at the manor and folded her arms across her chest.

Una opened her mouth to argue, but before she could get the words out Turlouch interrupted, "There's no time to come in and be sociable. We have to get back before the storm. We'd hoped to find you and Miss Mara here earlier when we came. Walk with us down to the peir and we'll tell you the news."

Una glanced at the sky as well, then reluctantly followed Turlouch and her sister down the trail to the boat dock. As the rain began Sean yelled at her to come in, but she ignored the command. "I'll be along after I say good bye."

WITH ONLY THE CANDLELIGHT and an attentive Adam by her side in the dining room, their hastily prepared supper of fried potatoes, eggs and beans out of a can, was pleasantly romantic nonetheless, Mara thought. Later when they were tangled together in Mara's bed, Adam's tender and passionate love was the climax of a most perfect day.

"I've been missing you desperately, you know," Adam whispered next to her ear. "Forget about the manor and the islands for a while. If you don't want to sell, I won't pressure you. Won't you please come home with me?"

Mara sighed. She really should get back; her classes would be starting soon. She could use some of her savings to pay the MacCarthaighs and the worst of Seamas's debts. The rest could be sorted out later. "All right. If it means that much to you I'll come."

"That's wonderful, Darling." Adam laughed and hugged her. Then all business again, he added, "While I waited for you yesterday, I made an appointment with a business associate Laurence wanted me to meet with while I'm here. Sean says you've things pretty much wrapped up. Why don't you come with me? You can do a bit more sight-seeing and then we'll have a nice lunch at a special restaurant I've heard of in Galway. We'll book our flight while we're out. And then we can leave the following day."

In the back of her mind a tiny voice warned, How convenient all these arrangements happened to be? Was Adam trying to trick her for some reason into leaving? No, that was impossible. *Too paranoid, Mara, get a grip!*

This house, the islands and that crazy Ronfear were the ones conspiring against her. Conspiring to drive her insane. Adam was right, she needed to go home.

"That's sounds like a great idea, honey," she agreed. "I just hope this storm blows over and the weather cooperates with our plans." Satiated, Mara was content. All her worries forgotten, she fell into dreamless sleep, cradled in his arms.

To her disgust, the ping of wind-driven rain against the bedroom window was the first sound Mara heard when she awoke next morning. Feeling lazy, she would have liked to remain in bed on such a miserable day, but she remembered Adam's business appointment and their lunch in Galway.

Already up and showering, he would insist on going no matter the weather. Reluctantly she through back the covers and hastily she put on jeans and a sweatshirt. Coffee, not tea, she needed some coffee if she was going to survive the morning. She'd shower and dress for town when Adam finished in the bath. Heading for the kitchen, she yelled through the bath room door that she was going for coffee.

On her way to the kitchen, Mara popped into the library to see if the day's newspaper had arrived. While reaching for the paper, she happened to notice a business card tucked into one corner of the desk blotter. The card was from Mr. John O'Cailigh of O'Cailigh and MacGrath Realty. Card and paper in hand, Mara headed for the kitchen.

The moment Mara entered, she sensed that something was wrong. Una was alone, but didn't acknowledge her presence. Mara smiled tentatively as she sat down at the table. "Good morning. Did you sleep well? Is there any coffee made yet?"

Without a word Una poured her coffee, then returned to her breakfast preparations. In that brief glimpse of her face, Mara noticed that Una had been crying. Embarrassed and confused she decided to keep quiet and drink her coffee. If Una and Sean had had an argument it wasn't her place to interfere. But on the other hand, if that macho bastard got after her because they'd stayed longer than expected in Galway, she was going to give him a piece of her mind.

As Una set a platter of steaming pancakes on the table, Mara put a hand on her arm. "Una, what's wrong?"

Refusing to meet her eye, Una shook her head and returned to stir the frying bacon.

"Nothing, Miss Mara."

Nothing. Well it wasn't her business; Una would tell her if it was. Deciding to change the subject, she asked, "Where's Sean this morning?"

"He went to the village. Is there something you need, Miss Mara?"

"Not exactly, I just wondered about this." Mara pushed the realtor's card across the table to show her. "Where did this come from? I never called this man."

Una let out a strangled sob and collapsed into a chair. Their breakfast forgotten, she covered her face with her hands.

Alarmed, Mara reached out a hand to comfort the woman. "Una, what's wrong? Is someone in your family ill?"

Not making any sense, Una blubbered, "Oh, we thought – but no, it must have been your man and – Her, the witch. Oh, wicked, cruel woman!"

"Una, please calm down and tell me what's wrong. I don't understand."

Una grabbed Mara's hand, squeezing it in her distress. "Please don't blame Sean, Miss Mara—he meant no harm, truly."

Mara gently pulled her hand out of Una's and flexed her fingers. She wanted to remain calm, but Una's erratic behaviour was frightening her. What on earth could have happened?

"Una, I know Sean is a good man, but what's that got to do with this card?"

Una sniffed and wiped her eyes on her apron. "The other day your man called a-wantin' you. Sean told him about seeing you holding hands with Ronfear down on the beach."

Mara smiled, thinking she now knew the reason for Adam's sudden appearance. He was jealous, how flattering. "I don't appreciate Sean telling my business like that, Una, but in this case, it turned out ok. We've made up and worked out our differences. I'll be flying home to Boston with him tomorrow."

Una's expression was suddenly guarded. "Leaving. Tomorrow. So it's true, then?"

Una muttered something unflattering, then seemed to recall to whom she was speaking and her mouth set into a thin, angry line.

"What's true? I don't know what you mean."

A flush mottled Una's cheeks and her voice sharpened. "In spite of your pretty face and kind words, you're unworthy of the trust your sainted uncle placed in you. You've betrayed us all. You're just like the evil witch that bore you!"

Mara reeled back in her chair as if struck. She was flabbergasted by the verbal assault. Her own temper igniting, she snarled, "Now wait just a damned minute! I haven't done anything – and I have no idea what's got you so upset."

"You know – you must know!"

"Well I don't." Mara took a deep breath, before saying more angry words she might later regret. Starting over, she said in a calmer voice, "Una, I'm missing something here. I have no idea what you are talking about. Calm down and tell me what's happened."

Still glaring, Una nodded and began again. "While you and I were in Galway, Sean says that your man shows up with a realtor and another man. Mr. Bensen says things are all arranged. Sean takes them to Inis Gheal, to have a look at the property. And while there, the realtor tells the tenants that they should start looking for somewhere else to live. My sister come over with Turlouch to tell me. Everyone's terrible upset, knowing they have ta' move. And the worst part is they think you sold the island – without having the courage to let them know proper like. I told my sister I didn't think you'd do that. But then you say you are leaving tomorrow, so what am I to believe –"

Una folded her arms across her chest, silently demanding an answer. Mara dropped her eyes, feeling betrayed and humiliated.

Oh, Jesus Mary and Joseph, is mama planning to contest the will, and if so, why would Adam be helping her? No, impossible. It's too preposterous....

Was Adam's gentleness and love the night before just a ploy to deceive her? Would mama and Adam conspire together behind her back? Maybe – but only over little things – that weren't important.

Uncle Seamas's inheritance was hers. Hers, damn it – not theirs. And she was getting tired of their meddling.

Returning her attention to the distraught housekeeper, Mara held out her hands in a pleading gesture. "Una, please believe me, I knew nothing about this till I saw this card. I asked Adam to have a realtor he knows in Galway try to find the Mr. O'Shea you mentioned. But I never said anything about selling Inis Gheal. I would never do that without telling you and the tenants." Her voice harsh with emotion, she added, "But I will look into it, Una. I promise. "

Mara snatched up the card and her coffee and marched off to the library. Quivering with indignation, she sat down behind Seamas's desk and took several deep breaths. She needed to get herself under control, before talking to the realtor. Just as she was reaching for the phone Adam appeared in the doorway.

"Ah, there you are. Is breakfast almost ready?" Puzzled by her murderous expression, he frowned and came into the room. "Honey, what's wrong?"

Mara put down the phone and held out the realtor's card. "When were you going to tell me about this, Adam, on the plane back to Boston?"

Adam sighed and flopped into a nearby chair. "Your mother and I thought it best to wait, yes. I should have known Sean or Una would tell you. I'm sorry, darling, I meant no harm. Last night I was missing you, and one thing led to another – please forgive me. I didn't want to spoil our evening together." He shrugged and gave her a boyish smile.

Mara wasn't placated in the least. "I see. You bring Laurence's realtor out here to show him *my* island and tell *my* tenants to find other living arrangements. What else have you and mama been plotting behind my back?"

"Mara, please. You're making accusations and jumping to conclusions without knowing all the facts. Nobody's been plotting anything. Gormla just wants what's best for everyone –"

"Everyone? Don't make me laugh. Adam, what did she say to you?"

Adam waved his hand in a placating gesture, but as he did, he also glanced at his watch, checking the time. Mara caught the gesture and knew what it meant. "Don't worry. I shan't keep you from your precious appointment."

Adam lowered his wrist, startled. "Mara, calm down. Your mother just said that I should pay attention if the caretaker was worried, about you and some vagrant who is hanging around. I told her you were far too sensible to fall for any rascal's line. But I *do* agree with her on one point. Your uncle's death has been quite a strain and you need to come back to Boston, so you can rest. "

Mara got to her feet, shaking with indignation. "Oh, you think I need some rest, do you? So the way you handle a threat to our relationship is to go behind my back, and speak to a realtor on my behalf, hmm? Bastard!"

Adam's face reddened and he got to his feet, glancing openly at his watch this time. "I'm going to be late if we don't leave soon. I just asked Mr. O'Cailigh to explore the market, that's all. We can talk about this in the car – or over lunch. Get your coat. We'll have to grab something to eat on the way."

"Get your own damned coat. I'm not going anywhere with you!"

"What?"

"You heard me. And, let me tell you – and mama, both. Uncle Seamas left his property to me. ME! I'll decide about the estate, not you – or mama."

"Mara, you are behaving like a child! Get your coat, so we can go."

Mara folded her arms across her chest and glared. "I said, I'm not going anywhere with you today. Go to hell or go on to your damned meeting. I don't care."

Fist clenched at his side he stormed out of the library, his voice trailing behind him. "Whatever, Mara. I don't have time for this now. I will talk to you tonight when I get back. Maybe by then you will have calmed down enough to see reason."

Then, before she could think of a suitably cutting reply, he was gone. The front door slammed and a few moments later a car's engine roared and drove away fast.

Muttering a curse under her breath, Mara glared down at the realtor's card anew. When her breathing had settled, she picked up the phone again and punched in John O'Cailigh's number. As she was passed through to him, his loud friendly voice asked how he could serve her.

"Good morning, Mr. O'Cailigh, I understand you have been speaking to Adam Bensen on my behalf."

"Hello, Mrs. Bensen, I'm so glad you called. I spoke to a buyer already this morning. He'd like to bring his contractor out to look over the property. Would Saturday suit you?"

Mara wiped a trembling hand across her brow. Too fast, everything was suddenly happening too fast – what should she do? "Mr. O'Cailigh, Just what exactly did Adam tell you?"

The man hesitated, then in a more cautious voice, he said, "Your husband told me, that because of the desperate financial state of the late Mr. Burke's estate, I was to find a buyer for the island property as quickly as possible. Is that not the case?"

No, damn it, that is definitely not the case. Trying to keep the anger out of her voice, she said, "Mr. O'Cailigh, the first thing you need to understand is that Adam isn't my husband. He is my fiancé. We have talked about selling, but I want to explore other options before I do that."

"Other options?" Then, adopting a patronizing demeanor, as if she was a child, meddling in the affairs of men, he added, "If the estate is in trouble, then selling the island as your fiancé suggests is the best option possible. What do *you* have in mind?"

Mara bit back an angry response, and answered calmly, "Well, the cook tells me that a Mr. O'Shea wanted to buy the manor house and convert it into a hotel. Do you know this man? Would he still be interested in the project?"

"Ye-ess, I know Thomas O'Shea. If you like I can contact him for you."

Suddenly Mara heard herself say, "I do. If it comes down to a choice, I think my uncle would prefer I kept the islands and sold the house. Try to understand, Mr. O'Cailigh. More than making a profit as Adam may want, respecting my uncle's wishes is the most important thing to me. And though the manor house has been passed down in the family for generations and my uncle Seamas loved it, it was the islands and the sea around them that claimed his heart and soul.

"If it comes down to a choice, I think my uncle would prefer I kept the islands and sold the house."

Mara's hand tightened around the phone, fearing she had just committed herself to an unknown course fraught with danger.

There was a long pause, then O'Cailigh said, "I see. Ah, the sentimentality of the Irish, it never ceases to amaze me. Well, I can certainly try to contact Thomas O'Shea for you to see if he's still interested in the venture."

"Yes, do that if you can, please, and get back to me."

When the realtor hung up, Mara tried to finish up with Seamas's papers, but she was too upset to stay in the library. Those poor people! She had to go to the island – explain to them how it was all a mistake.

Una wasn't in the kitchen, so Mara scribbled a note to let her know where she was going. Then putting on her jacket and a rain poncho, she headed for the water.

At the peer Mara untied the mooring rope, and climbed into the stern of the motorboat. The rain had slackened to a drizzle and would probably clear soon, she decided. Mara pulled the starter and the engine kicked over on the third try. She guessed Sean still hadn't had time to examine the motor, but it was too late to change her mind. In the next moment she was speeding out into the open water.

About halfway to Inis Gheal, Mara realized her impulsive trip was a mistake. Away from shelter, she discovered the chop of the waves was far more dangerous to such a tiny craft than she'd anticipated. The wind had picked up and she was starting to have trouble with the engine, too.

Mara began steering the boat in a wide loop back to shore as Seamas had taught her, but apparently she judged the turn badly. In the next moment a large wave slammed into the port side of the boat. The craft tipped wildly, and the engine died.

With the echo of the motor still ringing in her ears, she sat perfectly still and tried not to overbalance the tippy craft with any unnecessary movement. Alone in a colorless world – stormy gray sky above, angry gray sea below, under her lifejacket and poncho her clothes were damp with the fear sweat. It was cold and her hands felt like ice.

Stupid, how could she have been so careless? She couldn't stay here like this; the tide would be changing soon. She'd be swept out to the open ocean. She had to get the engine started and make a run for shore, before it was too late.

Teeth chattering and fingers numb, Mara carefully knelt in the pitching boat and reached for the starter. She pulled the cord. Nothing. She pulled again. Still nothing. Mara sat back on her heels and took a deep breath to calm her nerves. What was she doing wrong? Take it slow; think it through, she reminded herself. Sean had warned her the motor wasn't working well. The engine probably hadn't kicked over, because she couldn't get a solid grip on the cord from her current position. She was going to have to risk another move.

The rain was coming down harder, blurring her vision, Mara slowly shifted up into a crouch, grabbed the cord and gave it a strong pull. The motor burst into life with a roar. Suddenly, a huge wave came out of nowhere, picked up the boat, then slammed it down hard as it rolled on by. Hopelessly overbalanced, Mara cried out as she felt herself plunge headfirst overboard.

The chill of the water's impact sucked the breath from her chest. Lungs on fire, Mara kicked frantically, clawing her way towards the surface. But something was wrong, for no matter how hard she struggled, she kept sinking deeper into the green twilight. It felt as if a heavy weight had latched on to her, and was dragging her forever downward.

Stubborn, willful child, you deliberately lied to me. If you must die to save your immortal soul, then so be it. They will not have you.

Mara couldn't believe the words that came roaring into her fading consciousness. *Mama! Do you really want me dead – your own daughter? How could you?*

Then another voice, another memory surfaced. *No gills,* the Undine had said, *but your affinity for Water will allow you to summon the magic for a time, should you ever need it.*

Should you ever need it. What choice did she have; she was going to die why not trust in the Magic. Mara stopped struggling and surrendered to the power, welling up inside her. Opening her mouth, she breathed in the cool green liquid.

There was a long moment when she thought she was going to black out or die. Then her body adjusted to this new way of breathing. And as her breathing settled, the rage smoldering in her chest flared.

No, I'm not going to die, just to please you, mama!

Mara twisted round and aimed a punch at the creature she suddenly perceived clinging to her lifejacket. Her blow connected with a flash of white light, illuminating a shadowy form that seemed to be all teeth and claws.

The creature – whatever it was, howled and gurgled, but hung on. Allowing her growing rage to fuel her next attempt, she punched it again, then grabbed a clawed hand and pried it from her lifejacket. It roared in pain, flinching away as if scalded. Freed momentarily from its hold, Mara took advantage of its confusion, and swam with all her strength for the sky above.

Head at last clearing the surface, Mara sucked in great lungfuls of air, cold and stinging, but blessedly sweet nonetheless. Then treading water, she searched desperately for the boat, before the creature that had attacked her gathered its wits and tried again. But to her dismay, the boat was nowhere in sight – gone. Engine going full tilt, it had fled into the storm.

As the minutes passed and the wind and rain blew about her, Mara tried to keep up her courage. She was still alive, but the Undine hadn't said anything about her newly awakened gift helping her withstand the cold. She was freezing, half drowned in the ocean off the west coast of Ireland, and in spite of all her hopes to the contrary, she was probably going to die like her mother wanted.

Mara started swimming towards the gray shore she could make out through the rain, but already her limbs were growing numb, and she was so very, very tired.

"Oh, Ronfear, I'm so sorry. I told the realtor I wouldn't sell, but now it's too late, and I won't be able to stop mama and Adam... Ronfear, where are you? I need you."

It was so cold; Mara couldn't feel her legs – there wasn't any use in swimming. Her life jacket supporting her, she bobbed like a cork upon the waves. The grayness of the sea enfolded her like a cocoon. She was so tired.

Don't let go, my girl; trust in them. There is always the fairy magic to help you.

"Uncle Seamas? I'm so sorry. I've failed you, too."

Then, a sleek grey seal bumped against her sluggish body. Concerned dark eyes peered into hers; a black nose sniffed, and nuzzled. Mara reached out to the seal weakly, trying to wrap her heavy arm around its slippery neck. The seal pushed its head against her, then took the strap of her lifejacket in its teeth. Other seals grabbed portions of her clothing and together they pulled her along with them.

"Mara, mo chroigh, hold on, don't leave us now. Soon you'll be safe and warm."

In her mind Mara thought she heard someone talking to her, but who? Uncle Seamas's ghost again? No. One of the seals? Oh, she was too tired to figure it out.

Somewhere ahead, she heard the sound of waves breaking against a rocky shore. Then her flippered companions were urging her through the surf to the beach beyond. Mara tried to stand, but her legs were too numb She could only crawl a short way on her belly. She was out of the water, safe from drowning, but the wind cut through her soaked clothing like a knife. So cold; and she just couldn't go any farther.

Then strong human arms were around her, lifting her, and carrying her to safety. With a sigh of relief, Mara allowed the blackness to claim her at last.

THE FIRST THING UPON awakening Mara noticed was a faint odor combining fish, rotting seaweed, and a musky but pleasant animal scent. From somewhere in the darkness beyond her view, came the rhythmic sound of the surf. A cave, had she somehow found her way into a sea cave?

A bed of sand and soft debris was spread beneath her. A furry thing, like a blanket, covered her naked body. Just below her resting place water lapped gently against the shelf. Reflected sunlight from outside cast an emerald green light on the rock ceiling over her head. Mara watched the flickering patterns for a while and tried to make sense out of her strange surroundings.

Then another fact registered in her sluggish mind. She wasn't alone, the skin of another human body hugged her back, and a muscular arm was draped across her breast. Mara disentangled herself and turned round to face him.

Wearing only the silver shell pendant about his neck, Ronfear was watching her, his dark eyes luminous in the green light. As their eyes met, he smiled and bent to kiss her lips. She pressed closer against him, his warm solidity a comforting presence in this alien watery world.

"Good morning, mo chroigh, are you feeling better?"

Mara considered. "I'm not sure – is it morning – am I feeling better?"

Ronfear barked a laugh. Leaning over her, he took one of her nipples in his mouth, sucking gently. Mara gasped. He looked up, smiled, then sucked on the rosy bud again. Running his hand down her side, he let it come to rest over the mound of her sex.

His touch was kindling a fire in her blood. Mara curled a trembling hand in his long hair and lifted his head. "Wait. Before you distract me beyond caring, I want to know where I am?"

"Silly love, where else would you be? You're in my cave among the Seal Isles."

"But how did i get here?"

Distracted from his foreplay his expression sobered and he hugged her close. "When you fell overboard you called to me, and I came. It is a good thing you did, too. The magical rules binding me, would have made rescuing you impossible otherwise."

Was he joking with her again? Mara could feel his erection against her belly. Pulling back, she studied his expression. Was all this tempting sexual arousal only a ploy to conceal something?

As if divining her thoughts, he looked deep into her eyes. "I'm not teasing with you, mo chroigh. Later, when the tide goes down, Turlouch O'Murchu will come in his boat to take you back to the manor. One of my cousins has left to give him the message."

"Selkies – you still insist that you, and your – uh – kin, are selkies?"

"Mara, the knowledge of my kind is bred into your blood, your soul. You know what I am – you've known it all along. Why else would you have called out to me?"

"I-I don't know."

"Yes you do, my heart. The world is a place of wonder; don't cage its enchantments within the narrow walls of rational thought and social convention. We were meant to be a partnership – your uncle knew that. I am your true destiny."

His rebuke hit Mara like a blow to the stomach. To prevent her from lying with this creature, becoming his consort was the very thing her own mother would rather see her dead than let happen. Her own mother!

Mara buried her face against Ronfear's chest, sobbing. "Mara, my heart, my love, what's wrong?" Sounding a bit desperate when she couldn't stop crying long enough to answer, he cried "Please talk to me. What did I do?"

Mara shook her head. "N-nothing. It isn't you. Oh, Ronfear, she tried to kill me – my own mother – how could she?"

Ronfear hugged her close, soothing her with the melodic cadence of his voice, but the face she couldn't see was hard as stone. "There, there, mo chroigh, 'tis a hard truth you be knowing. I'm so, so sorry. I would have spared you that if I could. But not to worry. It's over now, and won't happen again – I promise."

"But why? How could she say she loved me and maybe kill my father and try to kill me too? Why?"

Ronfear kissed the tears from her cheeks. "Many of the things humans do are beyond my kenning. But you are safe with me now. Don't cry, my love, please don't."

Mara lifted her tear-stained face, her eyes wide with horror. "Oh, Ronfear, what will I do if she sends that horrible creature after me again? I don't know if I would have the strength or the courage to battle it once more. She's my own mother!"

In the shadows beyond Mara's notice, the Elder glanced over at them. He and his son exchanged a silent communication. Then the old selkie rose, assumed his seal form and dropped into the water with a loud splash.

Mara jumped. "What was that?"

Ronfear brushed strands of damp hair from her brow and cooed, "Nothing to worry you, my heart. My father just awakened and decided to go for a swim."

She sniffed and looked over her shoulder, but saw only the fading ripples of the selkie's passing. "Your father?" Mara blushed, suddenly reminded of her nakedness, and wondered how many other watching eyes there were in the shadows.

Ronfear seemed to sense her nervousness and reassured her, "We are quite alone now. Father has gone to conjure a protective spell for us. Be easy in your mind. No Ban-Feasa will trouble you again. You have the protection of the Sea Folk to guard you now."

Selkies. She was lying in a sea cave next to a selkie, had she died? But if so, was this her heaven – or hell? No, by the way he made her body feel, Mara was sure that she was very much alive. And Ronfear was right; she had known all along what he was, and she needed to stop playing games and accept that truth.

At that moment, his animal allure was very tempting. She would like nothing better than to stay in their watery little hide away and make love forever, but later would she regret her hasty decision? And what about Adam, her job – everything she had achieved for herself in Boston? Perhaps she was more her mother's daughter, than she would like to admit.

"You were right, I could never sell Inis Gheal. But thanks to," a sob, "my mother, I didn't grow up in Ireland. I doubt if I would be any good at this guardian thing. I have no training for it. Maybe I should just sign over my inheritance to your little daughter."

He silenced her with his kisses. "Hush now, I would be sore disappointed if you were to do that. Eire and this coast need a mature woman to care for it, not a babe. I can teach you what you need to know, mo chroigh. You have the gift. Trust in the magic. That's all you need do from now on."

"I'm serious I won't sell, but I have obligations in Boston, too. My job –"

Ronfear barked a derisive laugh. "Yes, a job in Boston – where your mother lives." Seeing her crushed expression, he softened his next words. "For a time, perhaps, you will have to go across the sea, but when you return, I'll be here waiting."

His reference to the threat her own mother now posed to her safety rankled, no matter it's truth. Not ready to give in so easily, she changed her front of attack. "You'll be waiting, right. But maybe I have no wish to be just another of your many conquests."

Ronfear opened his mouth, then closed it again. As if sizing up his adversary anew, he took a deep breath, and said, "In my ignorance, I have said something to annoy you. For that I am sorry. I'm not sure what stories you have heard about me, but Mara don't try to judge me by human standards. I can offer you love, children and I think, a fulfilling life. But I can't marry you in a church. It isn't a search for other mates that would take me from your side. I am one of the guardians of this coast and I must be free to fulfill my oath."

"Well, you're being honest at least. But can I accept your love on those terms." She shook her head. "Maybe I am more my mother's daughter than I care to admit. Right now I want nothing better than to be here with you – loving you. But I have to ask myself if I will feel the same way in a year or five or ten. Adam and I have problems, but as mama constantly drummed into my head, there is security in a marriage, and children need stability as well as love. I don't know if I want to be a single parent, especially in Ireland. I have some savings, and I can probably get a part-time university job here as well, but –"

Ronfear kissed her to shut her up. When he had her attention, he said, "You are forgetting about the treasures I can bring to you," he reminded her. "Neither you nor my children will ever suffer want. This too I will promise you."

"Tell me about your children's mother."

He sighed and then continued, "I found her pleasing, true enough. Seamas encouraged me to court her. He had no heir of his body and you seemed unwilling to return. You have heard that she died a year back, Yes? She was a distant relation of your family and I think your uncle might have made my daughter Ethne his heir in time, but his death was too sudden. My relationship with you would not be the same as with her."

He fingered the blanket wrapped around them, and smiled. "For you would have my sealskin. Hmm?"

Mara put her hand over his, her eyes moist. "You would do that for me?

"If you truly wish it."

Mara considered the offer, then shook her head. "No. I won't bind you in that way – it wouldn't be fair."

Ronfear let out the breath he'd been holding and smiled. "Your trust is a precious gift to me. Stay and let me teach you. With the power of magic to guide us, the bond we share will go far beyond the limitations of mere coupling. I need you. I can't care for the sea and its life on my own, even with all the magic of the Sidhe to aid me. There is too much about this modern human world I don't understand. And humans in turn need us to teach and help them remember the wonders of the natural world they have forgotten. To stand alone is to die – for each of us. Please say you will stay, swear the ancient bond and be mine."

Mara frowned, trying to recall if she'd heard about this "Ancient Bond" before.

His eyes widened with surprise. "Do you know nothing of the Co-Walker bond then?" Mara shook her head. "Ah well, that would explain so much."

"If I heard of this bond as a child I have forgotten. And mama – please explain."

"Hmm, how to explain. First you must understand that the Realm of Fairy and the Human World are connected. What happens in one is mirrored in the other. As the human world began to change, corrupted by evil magic and the pollution of human greed, Fairy too changed. Inis Gheal and the Seal Isles became one of the few sanctuaries where the power that sustains life in your world could be nurtured by those who strove to preserve the magic in both worlds."

"That's very interesting, but how does all this apply to me and my situation.?"

"How? Because your ancestor, Connor O'Ron, swore a sacred oath that bound those of his descendants through out all future time. He swore that in each generation one of his children in whom the magic gift was strong, would become the consort of a Sidhe. Together the two, human and selkie, Co-Walkers between the Worlds, would unite their powers and become the guardians of Eire and Mother Ocean.

"Your Mother had, and still has, that power. So in accordance with the ancient pledge, she was promised. She refused her charge, however, and your uncle who had only a willing heart, but no gift at all, was forced to take her place. Seamas tried, did his best, but Eire, and Mother Ocean have suffered under his stewardship nonetheless."

Ronfear brushes his lips against hers, then glanced up, his eyes luminous, pleading. "And now time spirals round, another generation grows and you are the one in whom the magic is strong. It is all up to you. Will you honor the ancient bond?"

Yes, he was right; it was all up to her. Tears stinging her eyes, Mara surrendered to the knowing, and answered the hunger in his body with her own.

WITH THE CHANGING OF the tide came visitors to their watery love nest. First to arrive was the Elder. Shifting into human form, he led Mara and his son deeper into the cavern. Beside an inky pool Mara knelt alongside her lover and took the oath of the Guardian and Co-Walker. At the conclusion of the ceremony she received a silver shell pendant, the mirror image of Ronfear's.

Not long after their return from the pool, someone hailed them from the beach beyond. It was Turlouch with clean dry clothes for Mara, borrowed from the women on Inis Gheal. He'd also come to take her back to the manor.

When they arrived Turlouch cut the motor and eased the skiff into the peer. Ronfear, in human form secured the mooring line and helped Mara from the boat. As he released her, he looked into her eyes. "Shall I come with you up to the house?"

How much time had passed since she'd fallen out of the motorboat? She'd forgotten to ask. And, what if Adam – or her mother were up there? Mara shook her head and took a deep, steadying breath. "No. I have to do this myself."

He nodded and brushed a kiss across her lips. "I will be near if you need me. you need only call."

"I know. Thank you."

After one last kiss Mara turned from him and started up the trail. Turlouch stared after her, indecisive. Ronfear motioned with his chin up the trail. In a voice barely above a whisper, he urged, "Go with her, cousin. She is being very brave, but she may need our support nonetheless."

Turlouch gave him a nod and hurried to follow. When they neared the closed kitchen door, He laid a hand on her shoulder to stop her. "Miss Mara, you would be welcome should you wish to come live among us."

Startled she turned to stare, making him suddenly shy."I mean no offence and all. I just thought you being one o' us now and Ronfear's – uh – we would build you a nice snug cottage, all your own. If you wanted to come."

Hand on the door knob Mara smiled.She had given blood oath and now wore the charm of a Co-Walker between her breasts. She had been *chosen* by a selkie, and In spite of being raised abroad, she felt loved and accepted, a part of their secret family."Thank you, Turlouch, I will definitely consider it." Then, opening the door she stepped inside.

Sean and Una were in the kitchen just finishing a meal. When Una recognized her, she let out a cry as if she was seeing a ghost. The plate she was holding shattered upon the floor. Sean too was shocked to see them, but remain sitting at the table, drinking his tea.

"Oh, Miss Mara, may the saints and the Good People be thanked that you are alive and safe." When she noticed the shell pendant, she touched it reverently and burst into tears. Mara hugged her close, her own eyes moist.

"I'm glad to see you safe as well," Sean said. "We feared the worst when we saw the boat gone and couldn't find you."

"I'm sorry about the boat, Sean. It was foolish for me to go off like that, but I was so angry when I learned that Adam and the realtor had been plotting behind my back. I had to tell the people on the island that I wasn't going to sell."

Una made Mara and Turlouch sit and over a hot meal, Mara outlined her plans. She told the MacCarthaighs she wasn't going to sell Inis Gheal. she'd use her own savings to pay their salaries and keep the creditors at bay, until the O'Sheas or someone else could be found to lease or buy the manor.

When they were nearly finished eating, Sean asked, "And what of your marriage plans? Will you and the mister be living here then? He was powerful up set when he come back and found you missing – maybe dead."

Una snorted and glared at him. "So powerful upset, that he be on the phone to that hateful witch woman first thing – before we knows if you be lost or just visitin' on the island. And then she tells the mister to call the realtor and tell him she wants him to sell everything, the islands, the manor, everything – right now!"

"No one is going to sell Inis Gheal, Una, neither Adam or my mother, so be easy in your mind. I will sell the manor house first if I have to." Mara sighed. "Poor Mr. O'Cailigh. He must think we are all a bunch of lunatics out here. I suppose I will have to call him in the morning and explain once again. I wonder what Adam told him?"

"You can ask him yourself," Sean said. "He's in the library."

"In the library? I'm surprised he didn't go back to Boston."

In spite of how her feelings had changed towards Adam, Mara was touched. For him to have set aside his business concerns, because he was worried about her safety, he must truly have cared for her....

Una's next words pricked her illusion. "Gormla wouldn't let him leave, until the real estate deal is signed."

Sean scowled. "Mind your tongue, woman. You don't know that for certain." Una gave him a defiant look, then glancing at Mara dropped her eyes.

Mara pushed her chair away from the table and rose. Without looking at anyone, she said, "I guess I'd better go talk to him. Tell him I'm back."

THE LIGHT WAS DIM IN the library. Adam sat with a half-finished whiskey bottle beside him on the end table. He looked exhausted. Mara called his name, but he didn't look up. Coming further into the room, she sat down in a chair nearby.

Without looking at her, Adam poured himself another drink and swallowed half the glass's contents before speaking. "Your mother and I thought you were dead. Did you know that? Do you care? No, of course not." He laughed to himself and finished the glass.

"I'm sorry, Adam, if I caused you to worry. I fell out of the motorboat and almost drowned. Fortunately some of the island's inhabitants rescued me, but the storm made it impossible to let you know. I came back as soon as I could."

He snorted and poured another drink. "There's been two days clear weather since the storm, Mara. Surely you could have let me know – if you'd wanted."

Two days, had it truly been that long? Well, maybe he had a right to be cross with her, but she wasn't going to change her mind just because he was laying on the guilt. "You're right. Maybe I should have done that, but I assumed you'd gone back to Boston. I'm sorry. I was in bed for much of that time. I didn't know it had been so long."

"In bed, eh?" Adam let out a mirthless laugh and glared. "Just what kind of bastard do you think I am? Do you actually believe I could go back to Boston, not knowing what had happened to my fiancée?"

Mara's eyes flashed as her temper ignited. She was not going to let him make her feel bad about this, damn him. "I don't know if you are an unfeeling bastard. But I do know that you are the kind of man who would conspire with my mother to sell off my inheritance, before you knew if I were alive or dead."

Adam gulped down another large swallow of his drink. They both sat in silence for a time, each not knowing what else to say. Finally looking even more defeated than before, he sighed and spoke. "It's over between us isn't it, Mara. You are actually going to give up everything you have in Boston, marriage, a fine home, university job, and all for some handsome Irish tramp with a clever line. "

"Yes, I guess I am."

He seemed surprised that she would agree so easily with his assessment of the situation. Still trying to prod her anger, he persisted, "I thought you were smarter than that. I guess your mother was right about you and this place. I wish you had gone back to Boston and let me sell the whole damned property."

"Well, I'm glad you didn't. And don't talk to me about my mother. She's meddled in my life for the last time. I don't want to see or talk to her again after what she's done."

"You're mad, you know that? I wish we were married, so I had the power to have you committed."

That did it. Throwing restraint to the wind she jumped to her feet, fist clenched. "You bastard! How could I ever have been so stupid as to think I was in love with you."

Mara might have said more or done something she might have later regretted, but the phone interrupted at that moment. Her temper barely under control she snatched up the phone and growled a hello into the mouth piece.

Her angry flush paling, she listened to someone on the other end for a time, answering in monosyllables. At last she hung up with a shaking hand, staring blankly at the closed drapes.

"Mara, what's wrong? What's happened?"

At first Mara gave no sign that she had even heard him. When he repeated his question, more insistently, she tore herself out of her shock and answered in a flat voice. "That was mama's doctor. His office has been trying to track me down. Got this number from your assistant. Mama's had a stroke. She's in the university Hospital."

"Oh, Mara, I'm sorry. I had no idea she was ill. How bad is she?"

"She wasn't ill as far as I knew either."

Still reeling from the shock, Mara collapsed into a nearby chair, her face chalk white, her hands shaking. Adam got up, retrieved the brandy from a sideboard against the wall and poured her a drink. He placed it in her hand, she took it automatically, but seemed unable to bring the brimming glass to her lips. Adam flopped back into his own chair.

"Drink it. It will help settle your nerves. Does the doctor think she'll recover?"

"The doctor says she suffered a severe stroke yesterday. She's lost all movement on the right side of her body, as well as the ability to speak."

Mara let out a brittle laugh and gulped down a large swallow of the liquor. Suddenly she realized that there might be a more sinister aspect to the oath she had so blithely sworn, while still ensnared in the romantic glow of her lovemaking with Ronfear. Was this somehow her fault? Unconsciously she fingered the pendant around her neck. Had Ronfear – or the Elder – done this? They had promised her safety, but did it have to be at such a terrible price?

"Mara? Are you all right, my dear?"

"Yes, I'm – fine. The doctor is hopeful. With time and therapy she will gain back some of her lost functions, he thinks. But she will probably need the constant care of a nursing home from now on."

Adam drank, then set down his glass and stood. Before leaving her, he couldn't resist a last bitter jab. "More money troubles for you, eh, Mara? Want to change your mind about leaving me? What will you do now? Are you going home to see her? And what about your job? Are you going to leave the university in the lurch? Where are you going to come up with so much money, if you leave me and quit your job, hmm?"

Her voice devoid of emotion, she answered him calmly, as if explaining to a simple child. "This is my home now, Adam. But to answer your question, I will go back to Boston as soon as I can book a flight. I will have to make arrangements for her care and give my notice at the university. And as you've already implied, my troubles are no longer your concern. I'll manage – some how. Good bye, Adam. I wish you well."

THE SOUND OF THE SURF a quiet rumble below the cliffs, Mara walked into the shadowy garden and sat on a mossy bench. It was late, the house quiet behind her. So much had happened to her in such a short time that she felt numb. It was comforting just to sit in the shadowy stillness and not think.

Knowing he would find her, Mara wasn't surprised when Ronfear came up quietly and joined her. They sat in silence for a time just enjoying the night and each other's closeness. Finally Mara's need to know could not be held back any longer.

"Mama had a stroke. She's paralyzed on her right side and can't speak. Did the Elder do that to her? Did you know that was going to happen?"

Ronfear sighed and put a comforting arm about her shoulder. "I only knew that you would be safe, my heart, protected from her malice. Father conjured a lorica to reflect evil. If Gormla has suffered, then it is no more than her own spell turning against her."

Did she believe him? She wanted to – but... She leaned into his warmth. She had to trust him; if she did not, or could not, then there was no point in continuing along the path she had chosen. "All this is so horrible. I feel – I don't know what I feel. I want to hate her, but I can't."

He hugged her close and kissed her hair. "I am glad, for hate is a terrible poison to the one who invokes it."

He kissed her lips, then released her and reached for a canvas sack, lying on the bench beside him. With another kiss, he pressed it into her hand. "After what you have just told me, I think you may need this even more than I first assumed."

Curious, Mara opened the sack and found it full of gold coins. "Why are you giving me this? Aren't you worried about treasure hunters?"

"Not if you trade the gold far away in America."

Secretly grateful Mara put the pouch in her jacket pocket. How ironic that she would use Ronfear's gold to pay for her mother's nursing care. Ronfear put his arm around her again with a broad smile. His kiss was long and sweet. She needed every ounce of her will power to keep from letting herself melt into his caresses.

When they finally parted for air, she said, "I will miss you."

"You will be back soon enough, my heart." His next kiss was feather-light upon her lips. "And until then, you will see me in your dreams. I will be with you no matter where you go, never fear."

Mara kissed him in return more deeply, letting him taste her longing and the sorrow she felt at having to leave him. "Mmm. You also could get Una to teach you how to use the telephone and then you could call and talk to me in a more conventional manner." His eyes widened at her suggestion and she laughed.

"Maybe I will at that."

He reached for her again, but she reluctantly stopped him. "It's very late and I have to get some sleep, my love. I have an early flight in the morning."

"Sleep is it now you be a wantin'? Then I shall come make love to you in your dreams." He kissed her one last time, then let her go, chuckling at her startled expression.

"Can you really do that?"

He gave her an enigmatic smile. "We shall see, won't we, mo croigh. Sleep well, my love and do not fear. I will be always near to protect you. Come home to me soon."

Still as stone, Ronfear watched till she had disappeared inside. Before retracing his steps to the beach he glanced up at the house, feeling the eyes of another upon him. He'd been aware of Mara's human lover watching them from his bedroom window for some time. He had deliberately distracted Mara with his kisses, hoping she wouldn't sense the intruder as well. Ronfear's smile became feral, displaying his canine teeth as he waved a farewell to his rival and headed down the trail.

TO THE SHOCK OF HER colleagues at the University, Mara broke off her engagement with Adam and handed in her resignation at the beginning of the fall term. She moved back to Ireland as soon as they could hire her replacement.

Goaded by convention, Mara visited her mother occasionally over her last months in America, but the meetings weren't pleasant for either of them. Though hidden beneath her clothes, the glow from the fairy pendant hanging round her neck drew Gormla's eye, the moment Mara walked into her hospital room.

Returning to Ireland, Mara leased out the manor to the O'Sheas. They were a delightful couple. Inspired by the romance they hoped to recapture from the past, they did wonders with the renovations to the old house. It seemed to once more belong to the land, rather than being an eyesore like so many modern buildings were.

The MacCarthaighs were kept on as part of the staff, and some of the people on Inis Gheal were hired to act as guides for the guests who wanted to fish and tour the isles. Some of the younger women turned a neglected out-building into a little store, where they could sell the island's handcrafts to the tourists for a bit of extra money.

Rather than claiming a permanent room in the manor, Mara chose to have the islanders build her a small, but comfortable house on Inis Gheal. Hers was a simple life compared to Boston, but to her surprise, she found she loved it.

Someday she'd grow bored and then she would probably take a part-time teaching position in Galway. But for the moment, she was content to enjoy their love when Ronfear came to her. And when he was away, Mara had her neighbors, her new baby and her adopted children to keep her company.

Inis Gheal was a good place for children to grow up, far away from the horrors of city streets. And only there, Mara knew, could she herself and the children claim their true birthright and learn to touch the magic.

Magic of Crimson

The fisherman leaned against the wall by my door and grumbled, "All seals are thieves and soul stealers." He glared a challenge at me with those piercing black eyes of his, daring me to dispute his words.

Outside, waves pounded against the rocks along the shore. Tree branches heavy with rain scraped against the rough-plank walls of my home. Trying to be polite, I said nothing, waiting. He shifted uncomfortably, pulled the mountain goat blanket tighter about his shoulders and took a large swallow of his steaming tea.

The older of the two sitting by my fire, a heavy woman with a lumpy face and arm muscles like a man's, glared at both me and him for the interruption. "As I was saying, we think my granddaughter may have been molested by one of the Seal People."

"Was she injured?"

"No, not physically," the younger woman said. "That's why –" She broke off, unable to finish her thought in words.

This woman was a younger version of her mother. She sipped at her tea and glanced nervously about the room. Her eyes glided over the bundles of herbs drying in the rafters, my rawhide-and-pole bed with the bright wool blanket in the corner, and the carved cedar-wood boxes along one wall. "How can you stand to live out here alone? Aren't you afraid of them?"

The Ani'Ya'Ron, the magical Seal People, were hated and feared by all the fisherman up and down the coast. The older woman glared at her daughter, and the younger stammered a hasty apology. I took a sip of my tea to hide my smile.

The women exchanged looks, then the old mother set her cup down and boldly said, "Some say that you are kin to the Seal People, and that is why you have chosen to live on out here after your children left and your husband died.

If the story is true – then you are the one who can discover the truth of my granddaughter's strange malady."

THE ROOM WAS DARK, lit only by the ruddy glow of the fire. Outside, another winter storm sent rain hurtling down upon the cedar bark roof. I sat on a bench against the wall, a feather comforter draped about my shoulders to keep off the drafts. My sixteen-year-old patient, Shashil, sat on the floor between my knees, listless but compliant. Her oval face with its dark eyes and full lips was shadowed from my view by her fall of long black hair, but I had seen the blankness of her expression earlier. On the other side of the room the grandmother and mother sat huddled in their shawls.

My apprentice sprinkled a mixture of dried cedar leaves and other herbs over the fire and brushed us with a raven-wing fan. I inhaled the fragrant smoke, placed my hands gently on the girl's temples and closed my eyes.

As I sank down into my dream, I heard my apprentice drum and sing her medicine song. Swimming through the void, my spirit saw a rocky beach at dawn, gray mist still cloaking the green water in feathery tendrils of luminescence.

Alone during her spirit quest, lasting the three months of her initiation into womanhood, Shashil, naked but for a loincloth about her hips, walked upon the shore. Her black hair, loose down her back, swayed with the movement of her long brown legs. She had a willow basket on one arm and held a heavy digger like a walking stick in the other hand.

Unlike the tearful, dreamy vagueness I'd observed in the home of her relatives, this vision-woman was vibrant, filled with moon blood ecstasy. She raised her arms and sang to the morning. She laughed at the antics of young otters playing tag up the beach, heard gulls arguing, and sensed the swimming schools of minnows, feeding in the shallows.

Continuing her foraging, she checked her fish traps, dug wild onion in a sunny meadow and collected tender seaweed when she returned once more to the shore. As Shashil headed toward the moon hut she had woven for herself out of willow saplings, cedar boughs and debris, she paused uncertainly. The hair on the back of her neck prickled in alarm.

Up ahead a small creek flowed out of the trees onto the beach. While the rest of the shore was bright with sunlight, in this spot, the morning mists still clung thick and heavy along the water where an old log snag lay half buried. Setting down her basket, Shashil turned in a circle, scenting the air, like a bear. Should she retrace her steps, take the long way back to her camp? No. She had survived more than one moon here alone; what was to fear from a fog?

She entered the mist with her heavy digging stick held before her like a club. Blood scent was strong – very near – but not her own. She climbed the half-buried logs of the snag, then nearly stumbled into the water when she saw the bloody corpse of a seal, lying among the branches and seaweed of the snag. It hadn't been there when she had passed that way last evening.

Shashil was elated. Such a windfall would last her nearly all the remaining time of her isolation, if she butchered and dried the meat. Cautiously, she studied the ground for sign of the predator that had done this, but she saw no tracks but her own. That meant the seal had been attacked while still in the water. It had managed to escape only to expire on the beach. Shashil went closer. She would have to be quick before a bear or wolf pack discovered her treasure and disputed her ownership of the prize.

Wading into the shallow water, she touched the oily fur. When the seal made no sound or aggressive move, she concluded it was indeed dead. Flinging her stick to the shore, Shashil picked up the seal's back flippers and began dragging it onto the beach. The seal was heavy, but the thought of its rich tasty meat roasting over her fire leant her strength.

At last the seal lay on a patch of grass away from the water. Shashil flopped down beside it, panting. The day was hot; she was sticky with blood and sweat from her exertions. Tiny biting insects buzzed around her naked shoulders in an annoying cloud. She was hungry. If she made a fire right here, the smoke would discourage the bugs, and she could cut off some of the fat meat to roast, before starting the tedious chore of butchering the carcass to carry to her hut.

She rolled the seal onto its back and drew her knife, but what was this? The seal's heart pounded beneath her hand. Startled, she froze with knife upraised as the seal's dark eyes opened and ensnared her. A voice spoke into her mind. <<Please, pretty human, don't kill me. I am no seal offering myself for your cook fire. Help me; receive my blessing in return.>>

She dropped the knife. Was he truly one of the magical Sea People? To test him, she said, "You look like any old seal to me. How do I know you are one of the Ani'Ya'Ron?"

He bared his teeth and made a phlegmy bark of laughter like a seal. <<You are a very clever young woman. My wounds .. I haven't the strength to change. Can you wait until I am stronger, pretty human? At such a time, I will reward your faith in me with sweet kisses.>>

"Don't do that!" Shashil gasped at the tingling warmth growing between her thighs and struck the seal hard upon the chest. He let out a painful grunt and blinked up at her. "I've heard the stories. You treat me with respect or I will leave you on this beach for the wolves."

<<I apologize.>> His eyes moist with tears, he studied her for a long moment, then said, <<In truth it is a new experience for me being so vulnerable. Your knife is sharp, I can see – made of the new traders' steel, yes? I only thought to please you so that you wouldn't kill and eat me – >>

"I won't kill and eat you – as long as you behave yourself."

<<I will behave. For as long as you wish me to – and no longer.>> When she glared at him, he showed his teeth in the way of seals, but his grin was curiously human and beguiling.

It took some doing, but at last Shashil managed to get him back to her moon hut and put him in her bed of cedar boughs. She washed his wounds and covered them with a healing paste of yarrow and tree gum. Then she fed him raw fish from her basket and he slept.

When she awoke next morning a man, not a seal, lay beside her. A man square of frame and well-muscled. A man with long, brindle hair, sharp cheekbones and lips that looked as if they knew how to kiss a woman breathless. Banishing such thoughts from her mind, she threw a blanket over his nakedness and rose. This was the time of her spirit quest. According to her elders, she was to spend it alone—praying. ... What was she going to do with him? She couldn't just abandon him, but if the women came to check on her...

SHASHIL BROUGHT HIM seaweed and fish soup as his wounds healed. Each time she looked into his eyes, each time their fingers touched as she held out a morsel to him, a fiery torrent surged through her blood. She knew he was stronger than he let on, but continued to indulge him. She knew it wasn't Ani'Ya'Ron magic ensnaring her heart, but her own body betraying her. The musky scent of her permeated the air of the tiny dwelling, heightening awareness and working its female magic on both of them.

In the summer moonlight when they lay side by side, never quite touching, she couldn't sleep for thought of him. Yet she resisted her body's desire, and he kept his word and never used his power to force her to couple with him. To take her mind off her body's betraying impulses on those sleepless nights, she quenched her feelings in talk, telling him all about herself, her relatives and the pale-skinned people who had come in their big canoes to trade with the villages along the coast.

He asked lots of questions about the strangers. Unfortunately much of what he wanted to know she couldn't answer. And though she persisted in asking, he never told her much about himself or how he had come to be wounded and alone on the beach near her hut. His evasions frustrated her, but he would only laugh and change the subject. Which made her furious.

"You tease me and call me your Star. I have given you my true name as a sign of my trust, but why won't you tell me your name or anything about you in return?"

"Tell you my name? Ah, pretty human, we never do that. Haven't you heard the stories?"

Yes, she had heard the stories; she knew what she was asking of him. He would be risking much to confide in her. But she was taking chances too. Surely she had the right to know something of him and his life under the sea. Who was he; what was his name? Why was he here; how had he been wounded? So many questions needing answers.

Unwanted tears stinging her eyes, she wiped them away angrily and said, "I know you fear I would have too much power over you if I knew your true name, but I would never do anything to hurt you—surely you know that by now."

Sensing her distress, he sobered immediately. He took her hand, his eyes soft and luminous. "I know that, my Star. With all my heart I believe you. I am honored that you have shared such a precious gift as your name with me, but it is for your own protection that I tell you so little. You have been so kind; I want no harm to come to you because of me."

Did he know how her people felt about the Ani'Ya'Ron? Probably. "No harm will come to me because of you," she assured him blithely, ignoring the knot in her stomach. "My elders will be angry with me if they find out about you being here, but they will not banish or harm me. You can tell me about yourself and your people, truly."

He laughed softly and took her hand. "I wouldn't wish to anger your elders, but it was my enemy of which I was speaking." As she opened her mouth to protest, he touched a hand to her lips, silencing her. "Yes, my enemies may come looking for me even here – and I don't want you hurt. They are fearsome creatures with powerful magic, unlike anything known to your people. If they were to find you – that would be terrible, trust me. Against your will they might force you to tell them about me. Try to understand, my Star; I can't take that chance – for both our sakes."

"I'm not afraid –"

"I'm sure of that, my beautiful Star. Don't pout or be cross with me. When my enemies found me and nearly killed me, it was the power of your moon-blood magic that lured me here out of the chaos. If it wasn't for you, I would have died, because I was lost in their conjured fog."

Shashil believed him and was secretly proud, marveling at this wondrous power that was her emerging womanhood. She had given another back his life with her womb magic, and someday, her womb would nurture and bring forth a child into this world with that same power.

SINGING HER MEDICINE song to the gray dawn, Shashil left her lodge to forage along the beach. Her flow was heavy; her second moon cycle had begun in the night. She would have liked to stay in her hut and offer up her prayers, then return to her bed for the day. She smiled to herself as she walked. No, that would never do; there was a hungry Ani'Ya'Ron to feed, sleeping in her bed.

She wanted to surprise him with something special, so she took her net and fish spear to the mouth of Plenty Fish Creek. Maybe if the fish were kind and came to her call today, she could rest tomorrow.

The salmon in the creek were indeed kind and soon her basket was full. Still singing, she started back to her hut as the sun burned away the morning mists.

Near where she had discovered the Ani'Ya'Ron, an unnatural fog cloaked the snag and the water beyond. Her steps slowed; a feeling of danger once again made the hair on the back of her neck rise. Three shadowy figures walked slowly towards the beach. They were man-like in form, but their heads and bodies were covered in what seemed to Shashil to be a hide of silver metal. Smooth, black shell-like objects covered the place where their eyes should be. A long ridged tube obscured their noses and mouths. It hung down over their chests and made loud snuffing sounds, like a dog trying to catch the scent of a rabbit.

My enemies have powerful magic unlike anything known to your people. I fear for you should they find you. The Ani'Ya'Ron's words echoed in her mind, filling her heart with dread. Shashil took a deep breath, willing herself to stop trembling. He was right about his enemies being fearsome creatures, terrible to look upon. They smelled of darkness and burnt metal. Alive, but not alive – alien. It took all her strength of will to not run screaming into the forest.

They had come out of the mists from another world to kill her Ani'Ya'Ron – she was sure of it. Well, they couldn't have him. He belonged to her. Feeling suddenly as fierce and protective as a mother bear, Shashil set down her basket and faced them with spear in hand. Her movement had caught their interest, and they turned as one to face her.

<<Where is he?>> a flat, colorless voice said into her mind. The sound sent chills down her spine, as they no doubt planned that it would. Shashil bared her teeth like a wolf and raised her spear. "You don't belong in my world. Go back through the doorway. You have no right to be here. Go!"

A harsh laugh, then, <<We seek our enemy. That is all the right we need. The scent of living blood has drawn us. We will search until we find him. Get out of the way, puny creature.>> They took a step closer, water dripping from the metal joints of their legs as they neared the shore.

Shashil laughed, the power of her moon-blood singing a war song in her veins. In her mind she heard the words of the old grandmother who had given her the teachings before her relatives brought her here. *Use your magic wisely, child.*

"Blood? It is my blood you smell on the beach this morning and no other."

They stopped. <<We do smell living blood upon your body, but you do not appear to be injured. Therefore, we conclude that the blood scent is not yours but belongs to our enemy. You will take us to him immediately.>>

Shashil offered them her toothy smile again. "No, I am not injured, but I do bleed. It is the magic of women. Have you never heard of it?"

They paused again. <<No puny magic of yours can match our power.>>

"Ah, but I am more powerful than you, for mine is a magic that can create life – as well as destroy it. Come, enemy, know my magic," she shouted and threw her spear stained with her moon-blood with all her strength at the one in the middle.

The blood-coated spear hit her adversary square in the chest. The monster shrieked, exploding into a ball of crimson fire. Shashil whooped and hurled a missile of magically-charged moss. Once more, it found a target, and another of the creatures burst into flame and disappeared. But before she could conjure more power, the third of her opponents faded back into the mists.

Amazed at her own bravado, her body trembling with the aftershock of the encounter, Shashil picked up her basket and hurried up the beach away from her hut. At the next creek she came to, she walked upstream in the icy water till her feet were numb. Then she climbed out on a bridge of rocks and headed off through the forest. She had decided to disguise her trail and take the long way back to her hut. If the third alien creature chose to reappear and follow her, she wouldn't be leading it back to her Seal Man.

Dusty and exhausted, it was late morning by the time Shashil reached her moon hut. All was quiet, but she approached cautiously nonetheless. To her surprise, the blanket covering the entrance was closed tight, just as she'd left it in the early dawn. Normally by this time of day, he would have risen, and pulled it aside to let in the cool breezes off the ocean. She paused by the entrance, listening for sounds of life from within. She heard nothing, and that frightened her worse than confronting the enemy on the beach. Had they known all along where he was hiding? Had the third one come for him while she was wandering about making false trails?

Stifling a sob, she dropped her basket and spear by the entrance and blundered into the pungent heat of the hut's dim interior. Then Shashil let out a frightened cry as strong arms enfolded her. When she recognized who held her, she flung her arms about him, resting her face against his smooth chest. Leaning down to kiss her, he rested his cheek against her hair. He held her tightly, rocking from side to side, crooning softly in a wordless language of relief.

"Oh, my foolish, brave woman-child. I sensed my enemy searching for me when I woke. I prayed you would stay away – and then when you didn't return, I was so frightened for you. I was coming to look for you when I heard your footsteps." Releasing her, he knelt and kissed the mound of her sex. "You are a wonder to me. The power you were able to focus behind the intent of your woman's medicine power was most impressive. I honor you above all beings."

She stepped away; he was making her uncomfortable with his praise. "Stop that." Returning to the outside, Shashil retrieved her basket and went down to the water to clean her catch. The Ani'Ya'Ron was a wonder to her too. Unlike so many men, he seemed to revel in her woman's secret mysteries. But even so, she had never guessed her blood magic was powerful enough to kill an enemy.

Later, over a meal of fish and wild strawberries, she described to him her encounter on the beach. When she finished, she asked, "I know you said before that you didn't want to tell me about your enemies. Well, that seems a poor excuse now. I want to know – in fact, I feel I have a right to know, after what has happened."

He threw the last of the fish bones into the fire and sighed. "Yes, I agree, you have earned that right. Though I fear for your safety should they find me with you, I will tell you what I can. Have your elders spoken to you about the mirroring of the worlds?"

"Mirroring of the worlds?" When he nodded, she shook her head.

"I'm sure your village wise ones would know; most shamans do. You can ask one of them for more details later. Very simply, what happens in your world is mirrored in other realities – other worlds."

"I don't see –"

He placed a hand over hers, stopping her words. "So impatient, my bright, crimson Star; let me finish. Your land has been invaded by strangers with iron weapons wanting to destroy your way of life, yes?" She nodded. "And because many worlds are linked, so has the world from which I came – and others – been invaded by the alien creatures you saw today. They too wish to destroy and replace the old magic with their new technology."

"But I thought the Ani'Ya'Ron came from the bottom of the sea. Isn't that just another part of our world?"

"There are convenient portals to other worlds below the water's surface which we use, but my kind don't live at the bottom of the sea as many of your people believe. But our worlds are linked by the portals, and because of this link, what happens to one happens to the many. Oh, maybe not right away – the time lines are never the same, but events have a strange way of repeating themselves from one reality to the next."

"Are you telling me that if the enemy in this other world wins control, the strangers from across the ocean will do the same in my land?"

"It is possible. The destruction has already begun, my Star, has it not? Even in your own short life time, haven't you been aware of the changes?"

Yes, she had. The priests with their foreign religion, the soldiers with their guns, the traders bringing whisky and sickness – yes, there were too many changes. There was no need of words; she was sure he could see the answer in her eyes.

"Yes, my dear one, and that is why the Ani'Ya'Ron fight so fiercely." Holding her hand, he rose to his feet, bringing her to stand along with him. "We battle for the survival of your world as well as others—never forget that, my Star." He kissed her hand, his lips a feathery touch upon her skin. "I grow weary and must rest; come lie down beside me. You must be tired too."

THE CHILL OF THE SUMMER twilight was in the hut when his movement roused her. He had closed the door-flap, and now was sitting tensely on the side of the bed, staring as if he could see through the blanket's brown woolen fibers like a window. Unnatural tendrils of a damp fog snaked through the evergreen boughs of the walls and roof to fill the air about them.

"What is it?"

At the sound of her voice he turned. One look at his face told her the answer she dreaded. He smiled to try and reassure her, but she could see the desperation and panic pooling in the depths of his eyes. The sight tore at her heart.

As if to himself, he said, "I am not ready. I needed only a little more time."

Shashil put a hand between her legs. A warm musky wetness flowed over her fingers. "I will go out and scare it off."

She tried to rise, but he pulled her roughly down beside him. "No. You took them by surprise last time, but such a ploy may not work again. I don't want to risk you like that."

"But we can't just hide in here and do nothing," she whispered, impatient with his caution. "You just said your magic is still too weak to confront it. I have to do something. I have to protect you."

"Protect me." His hand caressed her cheek. "Ah, my fierce one, never fear, we will do *something* – if you can trust me."

"Of course I trust you. But what can we do but fight?"

He smiled, showing the sharp tips of his canines. "Let us do the unexpected – perhaps the only hope of our survival." He lay back upon the bed of cedar boughs. When she still looked confused, he said, "Think, my Star, how else can you use your woman's magic?"

With the bloody hand he still held, he traced symbols of power upon his face with her blood. Shashil recognized the symbols as those a shaman would use to confuse and ward off an enemy's magical attack. The Ani'Ya'Ron smiled at her expression of dawning comprehension. Then the fear returned to his eyes as a heavy foot came down on a branch with a loud crack.

Shashil trembled, fumbling the belt loose from around her waist and eased the bloody loincloth from between her legs. They hadn't much time. She would use the scent and power of her moon blood's magic to conceal him. When the hand she placed between her legs darkened with blood, she wiped it across his neck and shoulders.

Reverting to the mind speech so as not to be overheard, he said, <<Yes, my Star, you understand. Cover me with your magic blood, my bright woman of power. Drown me in the musky scent of you.>> He brought her hand to his lips licking the last traces of red from her fingers one by one. <<Let me savor the rich taste of you, my Star.>> Raising his red mouth he allowed his tongue to slide across her dark nipples, teasing them to erectness. Shashil's body trembled; his caresses were igniting her with desire. <<Do you like that, my Star? Yes, I can see; you do like that – and maybe this? >>

Outside a loud snuffling began, then more footsteps by the fire pit. Shashil trembled, then mastering her fear, she dipped her hand and painted more of her blood in magical symbols across his legs and belly. On his chest, she rubbed her bloody fingers across his nipples in an imitation of his arousing caress. He smiled; his body quivering with eagerness. <<I am yours – always. You have won the heart of Cuan'Sleagh, my pretty human.>>

Shashil laughed deep in her throat. Straddling him, she lowered herself upon the shaft of his now erect male organ. "So, you name yourself the Sea Mother's Spear; I would test the hardness of your blade."

More sniffing and another footfall crunched in the trees behind the hut. The Seal Man uttered a soft moan, a new urgency to his movements as he thrust his hips upward. <<Swallow me up, my pretty human, yes, oh yes. Let your magic blood flow over me. Suck my essence up inside you with my seed, so there is nothing left of me in this world for an enemy to find.>>

Sweat and blood glistening on her naked torso, Shashil threw back her head and moved her hips in rhythm with his thrusts.

"Yes, oh yes, my love. I take you inside me.

"I will keep you safe inside me – forever inside me.

"All about us is woman's power, flowing hot – to cover us.

"All about us is woman's power, down-soft and engulfing – protecting us.

"No enemy will find us. No enemy can harm us.

"Bright moon magic protects us forever."

All through the night, the enemy prowled about the hut, but the alien was confused and never attacked. Throughout that terrible and yet wondrous, night, Shashil and the Ani'Ya'Ron who called himself the Sea's Spear camouflaged themselves with her blood magic and made passionate love.

Weakened and alone, with the rising sun, the enemy left off its search and went back through the portal to wait for a return of the night and the mists. Still entangled in each other's embrace, the exhausted couple sensed its departure and slept.

When the sun was heating the hut uncomfortably, Shashil awakened as Cuan'Sleagh opened the door flap. Turning, he saw her watching him. "Get up, my love, we have to wash ourselves, pack your things, and get out of here while we still can."

Shashil sat up, rubbing her eyes. She felt sluggish, her brain stuffed with cattail down. "Leave this place? Why?"

His lips touched her mouth, then his teeth nibbled playfully at her lower lip. "Because we need to travel somewhere away from the seashore. Somewhere on higher ground, where the enemy's conjured mists can't follow us. And we need to do this before twilight comes again."

She threw her arms around his neck, trying to draw him down beside her. "I am supposed to stay here till my relatives come for me. And besides, surely we will be safe enough from its magic. We were last night. Come back to bed."

His laugh was soft and musical, but he resisted her attempts to distract him with her body. "I would like nothing better, my pretty human, but later. Truly, we must go. It will not be safe for us here much longer. Can you not feel it?"

"Feel what? I don't know what you are talking about."

Standing over her now, Cuan'Sleagh looked down at her sternly. "Yes, you do know, if you shake the sleep from your brain and pay attention to your body. Your blood is waning. Another day, two at the most, and the flow and your woman's magic will cease for this moon cycle. By that time you need to be safe in your village and I need to be gone."

Gone? Her heart shuddered at the thought. After what they had shared, how could she bear to let him leave her? No, it was impossible, too cruel to imagine.

She allowed him to raise her to her feet, but still she resisted even though she knew what he said was true about her moon blood. "No, you can't go yet. You said last night that you aren't magically strong enough to leave so soon." Taking a deep breath she ignored the queasy feeling in the pit of her stomach and spoke the lie, determined to make it true. "If it isn't safe for us here, then come back to my village. My mother will welcome you into our home as my husband. Stay here with me. You will be safe."

He picked up a skin bag and began randomly stuffing her possessions into it. "Go back to your home? No, that is the last thing I will do. I will not draw those who track me into your people's unprotected midst."

In desperation, she cried, "But how will you manage, then?"

Dropping the now filled bag, he came to her and took her in his arms. "I will manage somehow, my Star, because I have to," he said and kissed her.

"Let me help you."

He studied her face, then nodded. "There is something you can do for me that would be most helpful."

"What?"

"Go back to your village and bring me your father."

"My father! He hates all seals – and the Ani'Ya'Ron. Seals steal fish from his nets and he believes that the seal cries in the night can lure an unwary human soul to drown as the person longs to follow them into the indigo world of the Ani'Ya'Ron. My father is the last person who would want to help us."

The Seal Man barked a laugh. "In this case, I think your father will forego his prejudice and be more than willing to help me."

IT TOOK THEM THREE days to circle round to her village through the rougher country on the higher slopes. Each night they lay tangled in each other's arms and made love. Shashil wished their time together would never end. Though it was the wrong part of her woman's cycle, she desperately wanted something of him to remain with her forever. So, with that in mind, she focused her will on making her body comply with her wish to conceive his child. And by the time they neared the village she was sure she carried his child tucked safely away in the warm darkness of her womb.

On that last day, Shashil put on her hide dress, hid her lover in the willow scrub along Hot Spring Creek and walked downstream looking for her father. He was often to be found by the creek in the late afternoon if he wasn't away fishing. As she'd hoped, he was sitting on a log smoking his pipe. At her call, he looked round, startled to see her standing across the creek from him. He stood immediately and came down to the water, peering across at her.

"What is wrong, daughter? It isn't your time to return; why are you here?"

"I need – someone needs your help. I won't break taboo and cross the creek, but please come over to me." When he hesitated, she said, "I am not on my moon-time. Please come. I – we need you."

Without more argument he crossed the creek to her. "If there is trouble, I would come no matter what. Tell me what is wrong."

For answer she led him deeper into the willows. Stepping into a small thicket, the fisherman jerked to a stop, startled by the man, wearing only his daughter's washed but stained loincloth, who rose to greet them. The fisherman's mouth thinned to a hard line when he recognized the dark eyes and brindled hair of an Ani'Ya'Ron. And his temper flared even hotter when his daughter put her arm around the waist of the Seal Man and looked up at the creature with adoring eyes.

"What are you doing here, soul stealer?"

"Father, please, he's not like the Seal Folk in the old tales. He hasn't tried to hurt me or steal anything. I found him on the shore wounded by monsters from another world. He needs your help to elude them."

The Ani'Ya'Ron stepped away from her and bowed to the fisherman. "I am very grateful to your daughter. But now that I am stronger, I must leave so the ones who trail me won't bring trouble to your people. To throw them off my scent, I ask that you paddle me far out in your canoe before I dive down into the other world from which I came."

His anger cooling somewhat, the fisherman grumbled, "I will help you, if only to have you gone before you cause more trouble. I will bring my canoe to the bottom of the creek. Be ready." Turning to his daughter, the fisherman said, "Your moon blood retreat is at end. You will come back with me to the village now. I will tell your grandmother what has happened."

"No," Shashil cried. Putting an arm about her lover, she faced her father defiantly. "I want to go with you and him in the boat. I want to help."

Slipping out of her grasp, he took her hands in his. "No, my Star, your father is right. You must go back to your village."

"I won't go back. I want to go with you into that other world—"

"No!" both the Seal and the fisherman said in unison.

"But you said my woman's power was strong—I saved you before. I can –"

He laughed, deep in his throat and hugged her to him. "Oh, yes, your woman's power is strong, but it isn't invincible. You could not survive where I must go."

She leaned against him, drinking in the pungent scent of male and fish that always clung to him. "Then let it be true what the old stories say," she whispered. "A Seal is a soul stealer. When you leave a part of me will go with you – be with you forever."

He looked deep into her eyes and read the truth of her words there. "Oh, my Star, I am so sorry. Truly, I didn't want this to happen."

Once more she hugged him, looking up into his enigmatic, dark eyes, willing him to accept. "I know you don't want, but you do need what only I can give you right now. As I told you before, I want to help you. If you won't take me with you, then I freely give my life's essence as gift. Take what you need of my power to make you strong enough to pass through the portal. For the sake of both our worlds, you must survive to war against our enemies."

He let out a long sigh, then acquiesced. "All right. I don't like it, but you are right; I do need your gift. I might not survive the journey otherwise."

"So, Ani'Ya'Ron, in spite of your lying protests to the contrary, you will be true to your foul nature and accept my ignorant, foolish daughter's gift of herself after all." The bitterness in the fisherman's voice made them look round. They'd become so intent on each other, they'd forgotten that he hadn't left yet.

His dark eyes pools of a secret knowing, the Seal said, "You are quick to judge me, before you understand all that is at stake here. But have no fear for her; I will be gentle and take from her only what I need to ensure I survive. And remember, in the months to come, I am not the only one who has taken something of value."

Curling his hands into fists, the fisherman said, "And just what do you mean by that?"

The Ani'Ya'Ron refused to say more, answering the fisherman's glare with an enigmatic smile that showed his canines.

Shashil stepped between them, and hands on hips glared at her father. "He is no thief; stop saying that! I am a woman grown now; I can decide for myself what to do with my life."

The fisherman dropped his eyes in surrender. "I can see that the damage has already been done; he has stolen away a part of you, and there is no point in arguing with you further, my girl. Like the rest of the women in your lineage, you are too stubborn for your own good," he grumbled. "I will get my canoe. The sooner he is gone the better."

The dream images of my shaman's trance faded as the lovers walked hand-in- hand down to the beach to meet Shashil's father in his canoe.

MY THROAT DRY, MY BODY stiff and aching, I opened my eyes and looked around the dim room. It was late, nearly dawn. The storm had blown itself out during the night while I journeyed in the trance. On the ground at my feet, the girl slept wrapped in blankets, snoring softly. Several more women had come in during the night, keeping a silent vigil against the opposite wall.

I wanted nothing more than my bed at that moment, but first things first. I would have to tell them the sad news. I could do nothing for the girl. A part of her had left with the Seal and would always remain with him. Licking dry lips, I softly called my apprentice to bring me water and help me up.

Later that day as I sat in the fisherman's canoe while he paddled me home, I looked out over the calm green ocean and said a silent prayer for the warrior who in some unknown world battled with others of his kind for our survival. I wished him bright blessings.

Turning to the fisherman, I said conversationally, "You never told your wife and her mother about your part in all this – why?"

He nearly dropped his paddle into the water with his shock.

"If you had told them about the Ani'Ya'Ron, there would have been no reason to fetch me from my home and pay my fee."

Not resuming his strokes, he placed his paddle across the gunwale to look at me. "You are right; I knew about the Seal, but I also hoped that someone with your reputation – and lineage – might have been able to cure her malady."

I sighed, seeing the pain and the guilt deep in his eyes. "You did the right thing in helping him. I know that is no comfort for what you have lost. She was a vibrant, beautiful young woman. It grieves me, as well, to see her like she is. You love her deeply, I know."

"I never could refuse her what she wanted."

I reached out my hand and laid it on his strong arm for a moment. "Be at peace with yourself. The herbs I left with your wife will ease her torment, when the nights are long and the Seal song calls to her. And after the child is born she may improve a great deal more."

His head jerked up at that revelation. "But how can that be? I knew they had been lying together, but she was bleeding at the time."

I let out a low ironic laugh. Men could be so naive. "You have unjustly called the Ani'Ya'Ron a thief. But it was your daughter who used her woman's power wrongly and is the true thief in this matter. Now she carries his child, a child who will suffer the torments and joys of such a mixed lineage. A child who will someday need my guidance."

Mother's New Sweetie

or

The Daring Adventures of a Scandalous Crone

It was dinnertime for William's men, and I couldn't help overhearing their belching and loud talk. The noise drifted up the stairs from the castle's dining hall, and through the open door to my chamber. They were saying something about ... Ralf the Super Stud? Hmm. Oh, come on, guys, I doubt if he could *actually* pole vault over the castle wall on his –

"Mother, are you listening to me?"

My son William and I were alone in my private apartment; he wanted to talk to me. "Of course I'm listening, dear. What is it?" He and his wife, Joan, went to court last week. Maybe Lord Thomas sent me another love letter. I wonder if William and that nice lord have agreed upon the dowry for my second marriage.

William is my oldest. With his long legs and square jaw he looks a lot like his dead father. He also has Walter's brown eyes and thatch of curly dark hair. I used to love to rumple those long curls, but after he grew up, he kept his hair cut too short for that. He told me he couldn't let it grow because his hair would get caught in that clunky helmet he wears when he's out "doing things" for the king.

When his look soured, I put down my mending, and gave him my full attention. But to my annoyance, then he clammed up and looked a bit sheepish. When I picked up my mending again, he cleared his throat, coughed, and finally said, "Mother, with all the noise my soldiers make around here, it must be hard for you to get enough sleep. And, I know the kids are always under foot and pestering you too. Joan and I have been talking and we think we can afford a charitable donation to the Sunny Valley convent on your behalf.

Now that Father's passed on – well, wouldn't you like to be in more restful surroundings?"

"Son, I may have passed through menopause, but I'm not in my dotage yet. All they do there is pray. No men – no parties – why would I want to go to such a boring place?"

Oops, I'd said the big "M" word again, and he blushed. Talking about women's cycles always made him so embarrassed. I never could understand where he thought babies came from.

"You'd love Sunny Valley, Mom, really. Joan and I stopped by there on our way back from court. The sisters are very friendly, and there's a beautiful garden to walk in, and the church music is marvelous – "

"In other words, Joan is tired of me in her castle, and the marriage to Lord Blubber-brain is off."

William grimaced, then hedged, "That's not true about Joan – she loves you dearly, and you shouldn't call Lord Thomas that, Mother, he is a very distinguished man."

Distinguished. Old men are "distinguished," old women on the other hand are "hags, old bats, or crones."

WELL, I DIDN'T HAVE to be hit on the head by a sword hilt. I could take a hint. Which was why, a couple weeks later, I was being shaken half to death in a stupid horse litter, while a small band of hired soldiers escorted me to the Convent for a "trial visit."

It just wasn't fair. I was maybe a "little long in the tooth" as they say, but, hey, even an old gal like me enjoys a little fun now and then. Why do most men want some bimbo with honey-blond hair down to her thighs that talks like she just learned to tie her shoes yesterday? Men! I had, and still have needs too, you know. And, I'm not so bad looking – for my age. My silver hair is long and silky. And so what, if my breasts sag a bit, it's only a few inches from mid-chest to my waist. I mean it isn't like they're hanging down to my knees or something. If my waist is a little thick, and my belly too round for fashion, so what? I had five babies, for God's sake!

I was thinking about the injustice of it all, when suddenly men were shouting and drawing their swords outside my closed litter. I pulled back the curtain a bit to see what was going on. Oh, damn, such a bother, we were under attack by a band of outlaws.

Shouting unintelligible curses at the ruffians, my escort rushed forward, but I could tell they weren't very happy about defending my honor. Things were looking grim. I was starting to get worried, then I thought maybe it would cheer them up, if I started yelling some encouragement.

"Yay team! Come on guys, give'em what for," I shouted. "Yeah, take that – and that!" Cling, clang, bam! "Oops, I bet that smarts." I was getting really revved up watching these doorknobs hack and stab at each other. It reminded me of the "good old days" when I was a cheerleader at the local tournaments. That's how I met my husband Walter. He was such a hunk back then, and so good in – "O – oo, whoa, stop!"

I didn't get a chance to see the end of the fight, because the horses carrying my litter took it into their heads at that point, to leave the scene. Scared half out of my wits, I hung on and hoped I wouldn't lose my breakfast before someone found the time to come after the litter and rescue me.

During our mad flight, one of the harnesses broke loose, and suddenly the litter lurched sideways, and dragged on the ground. I prayed the thing wouldn't fall apart before it stopped. The dragging weight, however, did slow the beasts. Finally they stopped, and began eating the leaves of a nearby bush. What a relief!

My conveyance was tilted at a crazy angle, but outside all was quiet. A few important questions ran through my head at that moment. Things like – where am I? And, who won? For a long time no one came looking for me – and that wasn't reassuring.

I was getting tired of sprawling in that twisted contraption, and about to get out to see for myself what was going on, when I heard rough male voices coming my way. Great. I thought, rescue at last. I peeked out through a crack in the curtains...

Damn. The bandits won.

As they came nearer they were saying some macho stuff about rich babes, and how many times they could "get it up." I smiled to myself, and straightened my veil.

One of the hairy brutes with a sinister chuckle poked his head inside the curtain. There was a wicked gleam in his eye and a lustful smile on his dirty face, but when he saw me, his expression changed. Poor boob, he looked like a kid after the bully just stole his candy. I laughed. "I'm not what you expected, eh, boyo? Too bad. But if you wash a bit of that dirt off, I wouldn't mind – "

He said something to me that shouldn't be spoken in the presence of a lady, and ordered me out of the litter. It wasn't easy with my arthritis to clamber out and still keep my dignity intact, but I managed.

"Hey, old broad, you got any money?" their leader said to me when I emerged. He was fingering his long knife and he gave me a nasty smile.

"Nope. I was on my way to a convent."

"Well, I guess we'll have to kill you then."

Believe me, I wasn't impressed by his powers of deduction at that point; it sounded like a bad idea to me. But I knew I'd better think of an alternative fast, or he might do it... "Hey guys, no need to be hasty. Let's think about this a little more. I'm a pretty good cook. You fellows need a good cook?"

As they looped the rope around my neck and led me off, I remember thinking to myself, oh goody. I won't have to spend the rest of my old age on my knees praying at the convent. I'll spend it on my knees, cooking and cleaning for a bunch of loutish bandits in a drafty old cave.

I'D JUST ABOUT GIVEN up on rescue, when one morning, I was awakened from exhausted sleep by a loud roaring outside the cave. The sound raised goosebumps all over my body and sent chills running down my spine. By all the saints, I couldn't imagine what was making that awful racket!

When I finally got up the courage to peek outside I saw in front of the cave a huge gray shape, brandishing a big spiked club. Though a bit taller than a human, he was man-like in appearance. He had heavy brow ridges, a pronounced muzzle, and very lethal fangs. It was a troll, and he was definitely *not* happy about the outlaws taking up residence in *his* cave while he'd been on vacation.

Well, let me tell you, the fight was quite an inspiring performance. The outlaws spilled out of the cave half-dressed, brandishing their rusty swords, and yelling unimaginative curses. They reminded me of ants when their nest has been kicked. Ah, but Mr. Tall, Dark and Gruesome wasn't impressed. He took it all in his stride. Bonking them on the head one at a time, or in two's and three's when they rushed him.

Near the end, when it was obvious who was going to win the fray, I couldn't resist coming out to get a little of my own back on the outlaws. A stick between the legs at a crucial moment, and cabbage-sized stones dropped on exposed body parts, really slowed them down.

"Too much spice in the stew?" Whack! "Your lucky shirt not dry enough for the next raid – take that – and that – and that!"

Suddenly I realized that it had gotten awfully quiet. Stick poised, I looked back over my shoulder. The clearing around the cave was devoid of living bandits, and the troll was staring at me with a puzzled expression on his gray face. I narrowed my eyes. Was that a bird's nest in his mane of hair?

"I – uh – thought I'd give you a hand," I said, as I put down my stick and gave him a crooked grin.

He blinked, then continued to stare. Finally he grunted, and asked me, "Why do you want to help *me*, human?"

I chuckled, but under my dirty gown my knees were shaking. "It – uh – s-seemed like a good idea at the time."

The troll gave me a disgusted look, and let out a menacing growl. That wasn't one of my funnier jokes, in his opinion. Racking my brain, I tried to think of a funnier line, but my teeth were chattering by then. I could tell by the way he tightened his hand upon his club that he was getting impatient for a real answer. I had to think fast. "W-well, they weren't very n-nice to me. I was minding my own business when they came along, killed all my guards, made me their slave, and – and I didn't like it."

"Would you rather be my slave, then?"

"Not particularly."

Still holding his club like he meant to use it, he came closer to me. Wow! His smell was a bit ripe, and that was an understatement. But, hey, I could handle it. After twenty years of Walter's stinky feet in my bed, my nose can cope with any perfume the male animal can dish out. I looked up over the mound of his belly, and swallowed hard. It was a very impressive belly – all gray, leathery, and a bit warty. My own girth was dainty in comparison.

He scratched his mane, straw and old bird feathers flying; then he looked at me quizzically, and asked, "If you don't want to be my slave, why didn't you run away when I was busy?"

That was a good question. "I-I don't know." But that wasn't entirely true either. I did know – sort of. I didn't have a lot of stunning options to consider. So what was the point in running? Oh, I could have gone on to the convent I suppose, or I could have gone back to William and Joan's, but neither prospect seemed very appealing.

Hmm... A troll would never win a Mr. Beef-cake contest, and yet...

I took a deep breath, and looked up into his gray face and gave him a toothy smile. "Say, do you have a wife or a girlfriend?"

He blinked, and lowered the club. In his deep gravelly voice, he said, "No."

My smile grew even wider. I stood up on my tiptoes, and ran my hand down his swelling biceps and onto his expanse of warty belly. His size and power were definitely impressive, but I just knew he snored. Oh well, I thought, so do I; so he better not complain. "So, what kind of troll are you, hmm?"

"A rock troll."

"Hmm, that's interesting." I slid my hand a little lower. "Ooo. Oh my, yes very interesting indeed. Why don't you put down that silly old club and come inside."

As my hand began sliding up and down his growing erection, he smiled, tossed away his club, and meekly followed me into the cave. By the fire, I pushed him down onto the floor, lifted my gown, and straddled him. I began rocking my hips back and forth.

Mm, definitely a rock troll, yes indeed.

Later, when I let him up, he looked a bit glassy-eyed, but he was still smiling. His fangs were a bit yellow, but they went nicely with his gray skin.

"Now, I'm very hungry; I want my dinner," he announced in a deep rumble.

That gave me a scare for a moment, but then I saw that he wasn't looking at me. He went outside and returned with one of the dead bandits. Well, what do you expect? He *was* a troll; you must have heard all the stories, haven't you?

"You're going to love my fricassee recipe. It's been handed down for generations in my family," I told him. "Say, you don't happen to have any tarragon do you?"

IT WAS A LONG COLD winter, but I hardly noticed. Trolls are very hot blooded, you know. The winter passed quite pleasantly. My troll learned to cook, and became quite good at it, actually. Which meant that neither of us got any slimmer. And he was such a sweetie; he made me my own little club with all those pointy things stuck in it – just like his bigger one.

On clear days, when I got tired of keeping him busy with – mm – other things, we would go outside the cave and make snowmen. He taught me the proper techniques of head bonking. Evidently, female trolls don't have to stay home and dust the cave while their men folk go off and have fun hunting. Troll notions of a woman's place are very *liberating*.

Anyway, I had a lot of fun practicing smashing the snowmen all to bits with my club. And, I built up quite a lot of muscle in my arms – for an old gal. I looked forward to the spring. My Sweetie promised he'd take me hunting then, but until warmer weather I would have to wait in the cave. The winter snow was too deep for my short human legs.

WHEN THE SNOW FINALLY melted, other bands of outlaws moved into the district. They caused no end of trouble for my son and the king's men. And, just to add to my poor son's troubles, our obnoxious neighbor, Lord Donkey-Ass, started raiding William's cattle herds, and the farms hereabouts.

My Sweetie was right. The hunting was good, and the gourmet meals we cooked were even better.

One day, when the trees were in leaf and the flowers were blooming, the sound of horsemen approaching interrupted our – uh – afternoon recreation. I sighed, rolled off him and grabbed my club. Damn shame too, because we were getting to the good part.

As we hurried outside a troop of soldiers was just riding into view in the valley below. They were shouting and waving their swords at us. Some people have no consideration. They just drop by any old time they feel like it – without even sending a pigeon message first. And then, they expect a person to drop everything and be happy to see them.

My Sweetie and I had a great old time roaring and throwing rocks down the hill at them. Actually, I wasn't sorry we had to stop our foreplay. The idea of bonking a few *real* heads would get us really revved up for later. My Sweetie was such an *animal* when he got excited.

Then I happen to recognize the banner waving over their heads and the tabard of the leading horseman. I put a restraining hand on Sweetie's arm. When he gave me a questioning look, I shook my head. "We can't."

"But why not?" he growled.

"Because they're family – or at least that big puffed-up idiot in the lead is."

"But, they've come to kill us... I want to bonk some heads, please, Snook'ums," he whined. "It's my turn to cook tonight, and I got this idea on how to put some new zest in that barbecue sauce of your Mother's. I want to try it."

"You do? She told my sister her secret ingredients, but she never would tell me – the old witch. Hmm. Nah – Sweetie, wait!"

While I was considering my mother's unfair treatment, Sweetie roared and started down the hill without me. Racing after him, I took hold of his arm and leaned my considerable bulk on it to stop his charge. "Wait, Sweetie, that's my boy William down there. Let me try to talk to him first before we kill him. I just couldn't eat a family member. And, you wouldn't want to make your little poopsy-woopsy cry would you?"

Sweetie glanced wistfully at the approaching men, scratched his head, and got this sorrowful look in his red eyes. "No."

Poor dear, he was looking forward to a good fray – fabulous sex – and a tasty meal. Before he had time to change his mind, I lowered my club and stepped in front of him. In my best "give me no nonsense" mother's voice, I yelled down the hill, "William, what do you think you're doing? Stop this right now, before you get hurt."

When he heard my voice, William reined in his horse, lifted the visor of his helmet, and stared at me with his mouth agape. "Mother? What are you doing up there? I thought you were in the convent."

"Well, I'm not. We got attacked by outlaws, and then the troll came and – "

"Troll! Don't worry, Mother, I'll save you from the foul monster," he bellowed. And, before I could explain further, he lowered his visor, brandished his sword, and waved for his men to follow him. He always was a stubborn little brat – never *would* listen to his Mother.

Beside me, I heard Sweetie chortling with glee. "He's not listening. I think we're going to have to do some head bonking anyway." He lifted his club, and licked his lips in anticipation. "It's a touch of mint and wild ginger that the sauce needs I think, and maybe a little more honey."

I stared at him, incredulous. "Mint and wild ginger? I think you're right – why didn't I think of that?"

Then I remembered my idiot of a son and the horsemen charging us. I ran forward again and shook my club at them angrily. "DAMN IT, WILLIAM, STOP THIS RIGHT NOW! You big boob, *save* me? From what – or who?"

William brought his horse to a screeching halt, so he wouldn't run me down, and threw up his hand to halt the charge a second time. He opened his visor again. "What are you doing, Mother? Get out of the way. As a knight of the king, I'm going to save you from that ugly troll behind you. Has he hurt you? If he has, I'll –"

Well, by that time I was fed up with his silliness, so I cut him off in mid rant. "William, your knightly duty has nothing to do with this. What are you babbling about? No, my Sweetie hasn't hurt me. Ugly troll indeed, is that any way to talk about your new stepfather-to-be?"

"My new *what*? Mother, are you out of your mind?" Then his eyes opened wide, as if he actually *saw* me for the first time. He took in my peach-fuzz beard, the sleeveless leather dress that showed off my new arm muscles, and the club in my hand.

Right then he would have made a beautiful statue for the pigeons to shit upon outside the king's palace. "No," I told him, "I'm not crazy at all. Sweetie and I are getting married – on Beltane."

The paralysis was wearing off by then so I hurried on before he could interrupt me. "Oh, I know this is a shock for you dear, but you'll get used to it. We've got it all planned. One of the forest pixies will do the honors. We were going to ask Father Murphy, but then I remembered—poor man—he hates to go out in the forest at night. The damp bothers his arthritis so bad, you know.

"It'll be a great party. You and Joan—all the family are invited. Just remember to leave your sword and armor home, dear. The fairies don't like to be around so much steel. It gives them terrible headaches, you see."

It's so tiresome when my grown-up children forget that I too am an adult with the right to make my own choices about my life.

My troll wasn't very happy about how things turned out either. He kept growling, shaking his club, and pouting. Poor dear—he'd been looking forward to surprising me with the new recipe. After I persuaded William to give us a cow as an early wedding present, however, he settled down, and was more agreeable.

Ah, well, everything worked out for the best. In exchange for William and his soldiers leaving us alone, we agreed to guard his northern borders from Lord Donkey-Ass's raiders. And if we take a few sheep or a cow now and then, when other hunting proves difficult – no one cares *too* much. Joan, and my granddaughter think the way I live is a terrible scandal for the family, but I'm too old to care about such things.

And boring family gatherings have become far more *entertaining* since my marriage. Sitting in my old apartment back at William's castle, I here the sound of someone climbing up the stairs. It has to be William. I'd know those clumping feet and that clanging sword hilt anywhere.

William's face was very red by the time he entered my chamber. I waved him to a chair. "Dear, you really need to get more exercise if you are finding it difficult to climb those stairs. I noticed there are a few more buckle holes in your belt these days. Perhaps a little more sword practice would – "

His face got a little redder, and he said through gritted teeth, "I get plenty of exercise, mother, that's not the reason –"

"Whatever you say, dear." I picked up my needle again. Was that supposed to be a rabbit, or a donkey with a fluffy tail on the baby's nightshirt? Joan never was much of a seamstress, so I had decided to help her out with the mending. Ah well, William assures me she has *other* talents.

William sighed heavily, crossed to the chair I'd indicated, and flopped into it. "Mother, we have to talk."

"What about, dear?"

It was dinnertime. I could hear the men assembling in the hall below. My Sweetie was down there too; he was the best belcher of the lot. He must have finished telling William's new cook how to flavor the gravy for the roast boar tonight. I hope the meal wouldn't be late again. Hysterical servants are such a bother, and William always gets so cranky when he's hungry.

"Mother, are you listening to me?"

A Dragon's Price

At the sound of the dragon's first roar, I snatched the sheet off the bed, flung open the door and staggered into the street. Knotting the cloth around my naked torso, I scanned the murky sky.

"Come back, my little flower," the old man I'd been sent to pleasure cried. "You've awakened my sleeping twig – you can't leave!"

I shouted in Trade-Talk, the language spoken by my people and the invaders alike, "No. You come out. Not time for kissing. Hurry!"

Suddenly, the thatched roof at my back burst into flame, and I stumbled backwards. The old man screamed. Heat exploded out the open doorway, blistering my exposed skin, and sucking the breath from my lungs. More towers of flame ignited around me as other dwellings flared in the street.

The dragon's roar sounded like a laugh. His sinuous body rippled with a metallic shimmer in the reflected light from the fires he'd started with his magic. His golden eyes aglow, his dark, leathery wings outstretched, his horned head lowered, tail whipping out like a long snake, he opened his jaws wide, giving everyone an impressive view of his fangs.

Pale-skinned villagers in baggy pantaloons and singed turbans ran through the streets yelling. Goats bleated. Women and children wailed. Gleeful Fire Spirits capered within the burning houses. They gibbered and taunted, beckoning me in the mind-speech with flaming hands. <<Come to us. You know you want to, Shamanka, come.>>

I shook my head and stumbled away. <<No! Leave me alone. I don't want to die. >>

<<Are you sure? A slave's life is harsh. We offer freedom.>>

A panicked sheep, stinking of scorched wool, raced towards me with its back ablaze. The Fire Spirits laughed. I flattened myself against a mud wall to let it pass.

Before I could move on, a bolt of white fire lanced out of the sky, and the dwelling ahead ignited, cutting off escape. A hiding villager screamed and disappeared among the flames. I staggered backwards, almost falling. Holding up a hand to shield my eyes from the heat, I turned, choking on the smell of charred meat.

I brushed at my tearing eyes and peered ahead, searching for a clear passage. Flames all around, smoke blinding me, trapped, I was trapped—no escape. I raced in one direction, then another, searching for a way out. I could taste the panic, vile and bitter, bubbling up in my throat.

Then, as if in answer to my silent prayer, I saw a tunnel of shadow between the burning houses to the left of me. With a grateful cry, I turned my back on the chaos, and sprinted towards it.

"WAKE UP, LITTLE FLOWER. It's time to go now."

"Go? Go where?" Still lost in the dream, I turned over in the straw. "Go way. Want sleep now."

Someone cursed and pulled my limp body into a sitting position. I slapped weakly at the hands holding me and tried to lie down again.

"She's drunk," a man's disgusted voice said. "Idiots! You were supposed to give her only a little liquor – just enough so she wouldn't fight us when we took her away. But instead, you goat turds let her drink enough to pass out. Where are your brains tonight? You know the savages can't handle the drink!"

Who was that talking – Belwaz? But hadn't he left for Farsa more than a ten-day ago? When had he returned? I smiled, thinking about Belwaz. He liked me, gave me a copper of my very own now and then if I pleased him.

"All is quiet in the house. He's passed out," the voice continued. "I have to get back; they are about to start. Get her cleaned up and bring her to the river – and soon. It's almost time."

"No. Want sleep!" When I struggled, someone slapped me hard and jerked me to my feet. I leaned against the stall and blinked the tears from my eyes. Then a blade of fear stabbed at my heart as a new thought pierced the drink-fuddled confusion in my mind.

I groped for the words, "What happening? Is dragon coming? Is more fire in village?"

"Shut up, you stupid whore, before you bring down more bad luck upon us!" Rough hands pulled down my dress, tied my wrists together and placed a wreath of fir twigs on my head.

"Nagril, why you do this to poor, poor slave girl? I be good. You want kiss me more?"

"Shut up and just walk," the thin man with hard gray eyes holding the rope growled. "Don't make trouble or you'll be sorry."

I allowed them to lead me out of the goat shed into the yard. My head hurt. Not long before, these men had been my friends, talking to me nice and giving me waskyja – good waskyja. Something was wrong, hadn't I done everything they asked? If I were bad again, Nadav would beat me – I didn't want another beating.

I glanced apprehensively at the quiet mud and stone house with its singed thatched roof. Where *was* Nadav; was he drunk – passed out? The men who'd given him money for my services, were stealing me away instead. Nadav would be furious when he found out – probably blame me – think it was my idea. I dug in my heels and refused to be pulled any farther until I got some answers. "No want go. Where you take slave girl, eh?"

Someone, maybe Fat Ranu, gave me a gentle push forward. In the darkness I couldn't tell who was there. "Don't be afraid," the voice soothed. "We're just going to another party. Lots of good drink there." He gave me another shove forward. "You want more waskyja?"

Yes, I did, just a little, to steady my nerves, but...

No, I didn't need any waskyja; I needed to, THINK! No one ever tied up my hands when taking me to a party before. My head felt like it was stuffed with cotton; but my instincts warned me not to go with these men. "Where Nadav – I no want go new party. NADAV!"

Someone hit me on the shoulder with a stick. I cried out and fell to my knees, breaking my fall awkwardly with my bound hands. Nagril cursed the newcomer as the rope burned through his hand. Ranu, standing behind me, said something in their foreign tongue that I didn't understand and pulled me to my feet.

By this time, more men had come out of the shadows and joined them. Always hot-tempered, Nagril lost patience with me and punched me hard in the gut. I doubled over, spewing the contents of my stomach on his boots. Someone laughed. Nagril cursed me in a low angry voice and stepped back, pulling the rope tight. They hustled me away, before I could regain my breath.

Yahweitsu spirits with pale a-symmetrical faces raced along side the tiny procession, jabbering encouragement at the men, and leering at me with their mocking green eyes. The vindictive little pests! "Go away!" I shouted at them.

"Nagril whirled. "Be quiet, or I'll hit you again."

I stumbled backwards, nearly falling. "I not talk you. Please no hurt poor, poor slave girl." I pointed with my chin to the grinning wraiths capering around them. "I tell bad spirits go away."

Nagril looked where I pointed, then gave a disgusted snort. "You stupid savage, there's nothing there. "He raised his fist and took a step towards me.

"Calm yourself, brother," Ranu said. Giving me a pat on the shoulder, he stepped around me and took the rope from Nagril's hand. "You go on ahead and tell Belwaz we are coming." Nagril glared, then stomped off down the trail.

Ranu pulled gently on the rope, his voice taking on a coaxing note. "Come on, Little Flower. Don't worry about anything you see in the shadows – or my brother's temper. Everything is going to be all right. We are going to a new party, remember? A party with lots of good liquor – you'd like that, hmm?"

No. I didn't want anymore waskyja—the Yahweitsu were scaring me. I just wanted to go back to my bed at Nadav's house and sleep. I tried to explain to them, but they hustled me along in spite of my protests.

When we arrived at the clearing by the river, I jerked to a stop. Terror clearing away the alcoholic fog from my mind, I stared transfixed at the man with the bloody knife. I couldn't see his face. He was only an ominous black shadow silhouetted against the fire, but I could see the blade. It gleamed in the amber light, long and deadly.

Someone jabbed me in the back. "Don't stop here. Keep moving." Ranu pulled harder on the tether and I stumbled forward. The hastily made wreath of fir twigs they'd jammed onto my head slipped sideways over one eye. A sharp twig pressed into my temple. In the shadows beyond the fire, my escort pushed me onto a mossy log and tied my feet.

I grimaced and covertly watched the villagers, mumbling prayers by the smoky fire. My mouth quivered, and my eyes returned once more to the man with the knife. Who was it? I finally recognized him by his beak of a nose. When Headman Jendil was angry with me, he called me a lazy slut and threatened to hurt me.

Tall firs masked the rising moonlight. It was cold and damp in the hollow away from the fire. I hunched my shoulders, pulling my arms across my breasts.... "I cold, me. Take me back Nadav house. This no good party, I no like it here."

"Be silent or I'll stick something in your mouth to shut you up," Jahem, standing at my back said. Ranu snickered.

And maybe I bite it off, too. The darkness hid my defiant look, but I prudently asked no more questions.

Ranu draped his cloak about my shoulders. I took in a deep breath and let it out slowly. I mustn't cry or let them see my fear.

On the other side of the fire, a low, makeshift altar had been built of saplings and evergreen boughs. The villagers had further decorated it with fetish items of alien design from their homeland. A goat lay atop the altar on its side panting, its legs tied together. It raised its horned head and bleated.

Blood of my ancestors! Forgetting about my bound feet, I tried to rise. Jeham slammed me down on the log before I could straighten. "Sit still." His scarred hands bit deep into the flesh of my shoulder.

<<Blood, blood, soon there will be lots of warm, tasty blood for us to drink,>> The demons sang to one another. They grinned at me, showing needle sharp teeth. <<We smell your fear, little human maybe we taste your blood, too, hmm?>>

The knot of fear tightened, making me double over with cramps. No, no, this wasn't happening to me! "Take me back or I call dragon!"

Without warning, one of the men smacked his fist against the side of my head, toppling me backwards off the log. I hit the ground hard, my breath exploding out in a painful grunt. Eyes wild, Skinny Nagril, jerked me upright, fist raised for another blow.

I was bluffing, of course, but the villagers feared the dragon *would* be back, whether I called him or not. As whore to the invaders, I was considered a traitor by the rebel clans, hiding in the mountains across the river. I feared my people's dragon-guardians nearly as much as the foreigners, but these ignorant villagers didn't know that.

"No hurt poor slave girl! I be good. Mercy, oh, mercy."

Ranu said something angry, too fast for me to understand. Nagril muttered a curse and pushed me back upon the log.

Headman Jendil's mother-in-law, a lean, hawk-faced old woman in a bloody gown thrust a bundle of tied herbs into the flames. When the tip of the bundle began to hiss, she withdrew the smoking brand and waved it across the goat's prone body. It followed the movement with white-rimmed yellow eyes. When So'yal was satisfied with the cleansing ritual, she tossed the unburned portion into the fire and raised her arms in a supplication to the starry sky.

In a loud, overly dramatic voice, she began intoning a monotonous prayer in their language. As she finished, the old woman stepped aside. Looking slightly ill, Jendil's son grabbed the goat by the horns and twisted its jaw upward. Jendil drew the knife across the goat's throat in a quick, practiced motion. The goat spasmed, its bleating becoming a frothy gurgle. Blood spurted from the gash and splashed into the old woman's waiting vessel.

Yahweitsu spirits swarmed past me to gobble up the blood feast.

I put my head down between my knees. I didn't want to see. The tremors running through my body shook me like an earthquake. I closed my eyes and mouthed a silent prayer to the ancestors to protect me – and curse these brutal villagers.

After the sacrifice, the clearing vibrated with an uneasy silence. The elemental powers drawn to this place were still lurking about unsatisfied. Out of the corner of my eye, I caught glimpses of gigantic, phantasms with long claws and hungry eyes, watching me.

<<You will be next,>> the Yahweitsu taunted capering in the dead leaves at my feet.

<<Shut up. Go away!>> THINK! I had to escape.

They laughed and capered about the foreign altar, their long tongues licking at the spilled blood. <<Think? No need for thinking! Isn't it obvious? They brought you here to die.>>

<<Go away before their god comes to eat you, too.>> the Yahweitsu vanished and I stifled a laugh. Stupid Yahweitsu. I gritted my teeth and pulled

at the rope binding my hands. My master would save me. He liked the money I made him too much to let them kill me.

The headman crossed to his mother-in-law, still muttering the last of her supplications. When she tipped the rest of the steaming blood offering into the flames, Jendil drew her away from the acrid smoke and spoke to her in a low voice. The old woman nodded, then asked a question of her own.

When Jendil answered, she glared, as if noticing me for the first time. "I told you before, headman, a whore would be an unsuitable sacrifice to gift the monster. It is written in the God's holy book that only a virgin can appease his ire. You were given money – my money to send your worthless brother to Farsa to purchase a virgin."

"And I told *you* at the time that it was impossible!" Jendil shouted. "If there even was a virgin left among these savages, every brothel owner in the south would be bidding for her –"

"You fool! I want my money back – every copper."

"That isn't possible."

The old woman's eyes widened, face darkening with her fury. "Why not? If you have spent my dead husband's hard-earned gold on another of your brother's crazy schemes to get rich – I'll –"

Jendil stepped back, throwing up a placating hand. "No need to fear, Elder, the dragon will trouble us no more. The money was spent well, I assure you."

So'yal folded her arms across her chest, unconvinced. "Then what did you do with my money, hmm?"

At that moment a loud bellow interrupted their argument. Nadav! My heart pounded hard in my chest. I shouted for him to hurry and save me. Jeham slapped me, cutting off my cries. Blood trickled down my chin from a split lip.

Jendil gave his brother Belwaz a disgusted look, and turned to face this new adversary. Nadav lurched across the uneven ground and stopped in front of the headman, swaying. "She's mine, damn you," he shouted.

"SILENCE!" The old woman shouted. So'yal pointed her finger at Nadav, then said something to him in a rush, her black eyes snapping. Nadav glanced around the clearing then laughed. So'yal drew herself up to her full height. Nadav made a dismissive gesture, cutting her off in mid rant. "Bah! This is no holy place. If there are any spirits here, they came out of someone's liquor bottle."

Returning his enraged glare to the headman, he said, "She's my property. Your men paid for one night of her services nothing else."

"That's a lie! The council has paid you for the savage—not her services and you know it."

Jendil's words slammed into my stomach with the force of a mule's kick. Sold me?

<<We told you, little human,>> the Yahweitsu jeered.<<You're next. Mmm, blood, sweet human blood!>>

<<No, no. Shut up, shut up, SHUT UP!>>

"Not enough; she's worth more," Nadav grumbled.

"Hah. You bought her cheap because of her tattoos and broken nose. You couldn't get a better price for her than what we offered," Belwaz said.

"Not true! She's a good money-making whore."

Jendil folded his arms across his chest, and stubbornly repeated, "You've been paid for the savage."

Nadav allowed his gaze to take in the goat on the bloody, makeshift altar. A sly smile curved his lips. "Hey. What do you want my slave for anyway?"

Jendil and his brother exchanged troubled looks. As the headman turned back to his adversary his expression hardened. "This is our business, and you will keep silent about it and be satisfied."

Belwaz grinned, showing his teeth. "Be satisfied, greedy pig, or maybe Lord Harukon's steward will find out about the lord's building supplies and grain you sold to the trader."

"That was your idea," Nadav bellowed. "And you and your brother shared in the profits of that little deal, too." He aimed a meaty-handed punch in Belwaz's direction. The still-smiling Belwaz stepped easily out of range.

"Enough, you pack of fools," So'yal shouted.

"Ugly old hag, go back to your sewing," Nadav snarled. "This is men's business."

"Headman, don't let him talk to me like that. Our God will be angry with us for the sacrilege. Do something about this blasphemer!"

Jendil looked from one angry face to the other and sighed. "Shut up, both of you. You're making my head pound."

"Hmph!" So'yal stomped past the fire and walked stiff-backed into the darkness.

Jendil looked in my direction, and said to his brother, "We need to go. The mercenaries mean to take her away from the village, before they set their trap for the beast."

"No! I want more money first." roared Nadav. Face purpling, he lunged at the headman.

Stepping in behind him, Belwaz knocked him on the head with a rock and Nadav crumpled at Jendil's feet. "Go to sleep, pig. You'll think better about the deal in the morning; when you're sober."

I jerked away from the man with his hand on my shoulder and leapt to my feet. Before I could hop very far, one of my escorts grabbed me from behind. I thrashed about, trying to swivel around far enough to bite. "Get up. I make you lot money!" I shouted at the inert man.

He ignored my pleas, lying unmoving on the cold ground. The cursing men, pulled my bound hands above my head, took hold of my legs and lifted my writhing body off the ground. I spat in my former master's face as they carried me away.

WHEN THE MERCENARIES dragged me to the clearing where they planned to stake me out as bait, I fought them with a fierceness born of despair. Aiming a kick at someone's unprotected groin, I cursed them for their cowardice. My dress tore as another man grabbed for my flailing arm.

With a laugh, someone ripped the fabric from my shoulders, making me stumble. A man with a scar on his cheek slapped me and I fell backwards. I tasted blood in my mouth and spat it in his face. They were toying with me like cats with a mouse.

Before I could rise, others grabbed my arms and legs, spreading them wide and tied me to sturdy stakes they'd hammered into the flinty ground. With their curses ringing in my ears, the mercenaries left me to hide in the brush and wait for the dragon to come for me.

Shivering with cold after a day and a night in such an uncomfortable position, a startled cry in the predawn grayness awakened me from tormented dreams. I listened, but the clearing seemed unnaturally silent now that I was fully awake.

Had I dreamed the sound? I wasn't sure now. My head turned from side to side, but saw nothing in the inky shadows. Feathery tendrils of mist lent the clearing around me an otherworldly quality. Somewhere upon the towering mountainside above a wolf howled. Stifling a groan, I stared up into the sky, watching the stars fade, dreading the day's heat to come. I licked a bead of moisture from my upper lip. Sweet – oh, so sweet. "Water, please, just a little water."

There! Another noise broke the stillness....

<<Water? Nasty, nasty, no water, only blood,>> the Yahweitsu teased.

My ears strained. Someone – or something was moving around in the brush near me. I was helpless – please let it not be the wolves. Where were the mercenaries?

<<Dragon will eat you – lots of blood!>>

I sighed. "Go away! Stop tormenting me, plea – " I began, but a shadowy figure suddenly loomed above me, murmuring for me to be quiet. I closed my mouth, my eyes opening wide. Had one of the mercenaries had pity and brought me a drink?

I could make out only a dark human-like form silhouetted against the paling sky. The figure moved out of my sight and fumbled with the cords that bound my wrists. Not one of the mercenaries then.

"No – "

<<Eat you, eat you, bad girl. Dragon will eat you.>>

My rescuer paused, then asked me, "You wish to die, then?"

<<Go away, little pests, before the dragon hears you!>>

"No, friend, but this is a trap. There are mercenaries hiding in the brush. They've come to kill the dragon and they will kill anyone helping me."

"Hiding? A trap?" The voice rumbled a laugh, then its owner continued with his task. When he was finished, he helped me to sit up. A tingling ache shot through all my muscles. One moment my body felt as if it was on fire, and then in the next, I was shaking with chills.

Without waiting for his help, I stood up. Then I regretted my haste as a wave of dizziness overtook me. I swayed and would have fallen if my rescuer hadn't caught me in his arms.

In the dim light he had a brawny solidity that was reassuring, but there was some quality about him that I knew instinctively wasn't human. I couldn't define it exactly, his unfamiliar musky scent perhaps. Or maybe it was the leathery feel of his skin – for he was as naked as I was myself.

Yahweitsu danced about us gibbering and clapping their hands with glee. <<We told you, little human. We warned you – eat you – eat you, yes, yes the dragon is going to eat you!>>

Dragon, now I knew him! My body shook like a leaf in a storm. One of my people's ancient guardians had come in his shape-shifted human form, but whether he wished to save me or eat me as the demons claimed, I didn't know. I was a slave, a whore – I was bait.

The dragon focused his unnerving, golden eyes upon me. Then he startled me by bending to lick a trail of fresh blood from my breast. Seeming to enjoy its salty flavor, he growled and pressed his clawed fingers into my back. His excitement mounting, he licked the bloody wound again, then laughed and drew me closer. I felt his hard male organ against my belly and my breath came in ragged gasps. Did he want to couple with me? Or, kill and eat me?

"Honored One?"

<<Not safe for you, little human! Not safe, ha, ha!>>

"ENOUGH!" the dragon roared and with claws extended made a cutting motion with one hand. The taunting wraiths vanished without another word. His temper once more under control, the dragon tilted his head to one side and stared at me. He brushed a clawed finger across the tattooed glyphs on my cheek. "Shamanka. I find your concern for me touching."

Touching?

In response to my trembling, his arms tightened around me. Unable to stop myself, I leaned my head against his chest as the spasms of shock and exhaustion shook my body.

Suddenly a wave of such despair and longing swept over me, that it left me breathless in its wake. It had been so long since any one had held me in tenderness. At that moment I missed my dead husband so much that I wanted to cry. But I choked back my tears. What would this glorious being think of me, if I collapsed blubbering?

Then, I heard his ragged breathing and looked up. He had forgotten me, perhaps, expressions of anguish, sorrow, intense longing flowed across his human features. I had no way to judge if they were a true mirror of his emotions. If they were, then like me, he had suffered some deep loss.

Big and strong, they were the land's protectors; how could bad things happen to them? But of course they had. Many dragons had died trying to protect our land. Some of them must have been his kin. Oh Ancestors, I instinctively put my arms about him in sympathy. I *was* of the old blood, and wore the sigils upon my face. It was a part of my nature to be concerned for his welfare and serve him.

Coming out of his reverie, he tilted my face up. My confusion must have shown in my expression, because he gently touched the sigils upon my cheek, with lips stained with my own blood.

"We should go." Pressing himself more insistently against me, the dragon held his arms about my waist, and exerted his magic to transport us elsewhere.

PITTED BOULDERS THRUST up by a long-ago earth tremor formed the walls of a natural alcove where we next stood. Near its outer border, waxy green ferns vied for the sun's light. Under my bare feet, a spongy carpet of moss and last year's leaves felt cool and soft. From somewhere in the hollow beyond came the sound of water splashing over stone. The approaching dawn painted the sky with vivid streaks of coral pink and mauve.

When I'd recovered my breath from the use of his magic, I asked, "Where are we?"

The dragon released me and headed for the water. "We are farther up the mountainside from the clearing where the mercenaries brought you – near the cave that I now call my home."

Seeing my apprehensive expression, he said, "We are safe here. We can't be seen from below." Looking very pleased with himself, he added, "But of course there is no one left alive down there to see us."

My heart singing, I smiled, showing my teeth like a wolf. What a joke; he had set his own trap and killed them all.

Taking my arm, he steered me towards the sheltered pool. "Come, you need to refresh yourself, and I will do some healing on your injuries."

Half hidden by an overhanging ledge, the pool nestled within the rocks at the base of a sheer cliff face. A small shrine to one of the ancient gods had been carved into a large boulder near its rim. The statue itself was weathered beyond recognition. A chipped clay cup and bowl lay in the debris at the god's feet.

As we stopped by the water's edge, I looked up, and saw a slender waterfall tumbling down from a crevasse in the cliff above. Its crystalline water collected in a large basin for a time, then disappeared into a small cave among the rocks. Where the bank was open to the sky, cress and horsetail grew in the shallows. The water by my feet was clear, but out in the center of the basin it changed to a jade green as the cavity deepened.

Its breath felt cool and inviting upon my tortured skin. I licked my lips, suddenly reminded of my thirst. "Honored Guardian, may I have some water before you begin?"

Crossing to the shrine, he removed the cup, emptied it of debris, and filled it with water from the pool. He handed it to me, gesturing for me to drink my fill. As I drank, he stooped and tore up a handful of the weeds from the bank. He dipped the clump in the water, and gently wiped the blood and grime from my body. I let out a long sigh as I felt his healing touch me.

The dragon both awed and frightened me in nearly equal measure. From a distance, or in the dark, he wouldn't have been recognized as dragon in his shape-shifted form. But by daylight I could detect the "wrongness" about him. Oh, the symmetry of his bodily form was pleasing enough, but other details were disconcerting. The way he wore his hair in a stiff braid that began atop his head and continued down his back, looked more like a leathery crest than human hair.

The color of his skin was also odd. A faint greenish hue underlay the normal brown. When he moved his skin shimmered with metallic highlights in a way no human skin could imitate. His face was even, if a bit strong featured. His sharp white teeth were very unnerving when he smiled. And then there were his eyes – dragon eyes – green-gold in color, with their vertically slit pupils. They were eyes in which the unwary could become lost forever.

Becoming aware of his partial erection, I flushed and looked away. In all the stories I'd heard of my people's dragon-guardians over the years, I'd never heard of a human dragon sexual partnership. At the thought of him touching me in that way, a maelstrom of emotions exploded in my chest. Excitement, fear, and maybe a little anger, too. He wasn't supposed to be like – like *them*!

I'd observed other women in the brothels of Farsa use a Woman's Magic to their advantage, but I had never tried it much myself. Most of the invaders thought me too ugly. And now, with my broken nose and the hint of age lines around my eyes and mouth, I wasn't sure this male of another race would find me attractive.

I had no basis on which to judge. But I had to do something to protect myself, didn't I? I was wise in the ways of men, but if He *wanted* me sexually, I definitely needed a drink of waskyja. When men wanted me, they often hurt me. Would he hurt me too?

Surely not – but all I really knew of the ancient race were a lot of old stories. Fear twisted in my gut, as an image of a burning village erupted before my mind's eye.

His expression seemed to darken the more he worked on my injuries. Unable to stand his silence any longer, I blurted, "Honored One, is there something wrong? Have I offended you in some way?"

He stared blankly for a moment, then shook his head. "No, Shamanka, you do not offend me." He ran his hand over a ridge of old scars on my buttocks. "I was merely thinking of how badly the invaders have treated you. If I had known you were being held in a village along the river, I would have taken you away before this."

I sniffed and swallowed hard. My own people had named me traitor – for allowing the enemy to use me – for not killing myself before I was captured. I'd always believed any dragon I might encounter would feel the same about me.

I took a deep breath and pointed to the sigils upon my face. "Honored One, I am unworthy. I learned what I could from my grandmother – and other relatives gave me their teachings, but I was made a slave not long after my first initiation. I won't deceive you about my skills, but I am willing to learn. Do you have need of an apprentice?"

His expression somber, he left off his ministrations and came to stand directly in front of me. For just a moment the dragon's golden eyes glowed with a strange feral intensity. He touched the sigil on my cheek again, then he nodded. "I do have need of an apprentice, someone to help me with my young – and other things. I sense your untapped magical ability. I can teach you, but consider well. If I take your oath, you will be bound to me until our agreement is over."

Consider well, he had said. I swallowed hard; his earlier sexual interest still unnerved me. Once, I would have done anything – even that – but such innocent devotion, died the night the slavers raided my village and killed my family. In its way his pledge was another form of slavery. Freedom or the magic, which did I want more?

"Honored Guardian, maybe I need to think about this further before I decide whether I can bond –"

His voice as cold as the wind blowing off a glacier, the dragon snapped, "I said I have need of you – now. My mate was killed by the invaders, leaving me to care for our clutch of young alone. I will teach you only if you pledge yourself at once. If you refuse my offer, I will return you to the valley below. You may supply yourself with the dead invaders' gear. Then you may find your own way through the mountains back to your people."

I studied his face, fearing he might be angry, or that I might have just forfeited any chance to gain the magical knowledge I craved by my dithering. Alas, I could tell little from his expression.

As a whore and a slave, I had ignored the magic's haunting call. I needed all my power just to survive. Untrained as I was, the little I knew before my capture was useless, so I angrily buried it with other memories too painful to unearth. There was no room for my childish fancies in my harsh life. After a while, when no war band came to rescue me, I stopped listening to the singing in the back of my mind. And when on occasion, the call was too insistent, I drowned any yearning for the magic, in a bottle of waskyja.

Making up my mind, I took a deep breath and knelt before him. "I want to be your student. With the Gods as my witness, I, Red Bird Singing, pledge my life in service to you, Honored One, until such time as I am released from this pledge by my death."

The dragon blinked, then stared at me in silence for a long moment. I dropped my eyes under his scrutiny, hiding a secretive smile. He hadn't expected a life vow. But I'd waited too long to gain my power to let him back out of the agreement as soon as his young were older and he had no more need of me.

Over the years, I had allowed my relatives and my slave masters to make decisions for me with disastrous results. It was time I took charge of my life and decided for myself. I wanted it all, and I was willing to pay whatever price was necessary.

Throwing away the sodden clump of weed he'd been using to clean my wounds, he raised me to my feet and with a clawed finger scratched open a half-healed cut on my shoulder. He licked the wound when it began to leak a little fresh blood. Then, with its salty taste in his mouth, he said, "I accept your blood oath, Red Bird Singing."

Extending the same clawed finger again, he punctured a hole in his opposite palm. When a trickle of blood welled up, he held out his hand to me. I licked, and as I did so, he said, "And, with the Gods as *my* witness, I swear to teach you, to protect you, and to care for you until my death claims me."

The oath taking over, we played like otters in the cool water of the pool. Then, when I became chilled, I allowed him to lead me to a particularly soft spot on the moss without a protest. I knew what he wanted, and I was petrified once more. All thoughts of using his lust to my advantage were forgotten. Well, maybe he would be quick about satisfying himself like all the others.

I lay down on my back and closed my eyes. I took a deep breath and tried to relax. It would hurt more if I stiffened up. I wished I had some waskyja; it was always easier when the men who wanted my body, let me have the drink first.

Waskyja? A dragon wouldn't have waskyja. How could I think of the invaders' fiery liquor while in the presence of one of the Goddess's sacred avatars? Appalled at having such a traitorous thought, I resolved never to drink the evil brew again.

Waskyja was a comfort to a slave, but it was evil. It made people crazy; it could kill. And I was no longer a slave. I'd better start remembering that and acting accordingly.

The dragon lay down on his side facing me. He ran his hand gently down my torso, exploring the curves of my wide bony hips, and full, somewhat elongated breasts. He let out a throaty rumble and nuzzled my neck. Once more caught up in his private reverie, I heard him murmur, "So alone... It's been so long."

I closed my eyes, discomforted by his frank regard, yet strangely moved by his earlier show of concern for my welfare. During the fifteen years of my slavery, no one had cared much about me – as long as I was healthy enough to serve and make money for them.

I could see evidence of his interest, and waited for him to take his pleasure with me. But he did nothing except watch me with his mysterious golden eyes. At last unnerved by his hesitation, I ventured, "What's wrong, Honored Mentor? Are you displeased with me?"

He sighed and gave me a rueful smile. "Nothing is wrong, Shamanka. It's just that this is not what I am used to. The matings among my kind are far different affairs. For us, the excitement of the chase, then the capture and ecstatic coupling in mid-flight is the way it's done, not lying in this hidden place on a bed of moss. Your female scent is pleasing, but the idea of coupling here is alien to my nature."

I was his first. He was a virgin – of sorts. I would have laughed at the irony of it, if I dared.

"Perhaps you will have to help me as we begin."

Help him? Not likely, I was too nervous for that. Maybe he would leave me alone, if I feigned ignorance. "I'm sorry, Mentor, I'm not sure how to help you."

His eyes widened in surprise, then he laughed. "What! Do you mean to tell me that you are indeed a virgin? Did those fools actually try to appease my ire by adhering to that old foolishness about offering me a virgin? Ah, little one, is that the way of it?"

The heat of my face intensified. His question shamed me. Why was I toying with him? Unable to meet that intense golden stare, I closed my eyes, my heart pounding. A tear rolled out of the corner of one eye and ran down my cheek. I was playing a dangerous game and I knew it, but I was so frightened and confused.

The dragon bent and licked the tear from my face. "I don't understand. What's wrong, Little One?"

I opened my eyes, blinking, more tears falling now. "As a slave, I didn't have the luxury of owning my own flesh. Over the years of my captivity, men used me whenever and however they pleased. What was done to me wasn't done in kindness. I am sorry. I don't know what you want from me." I took a shuddering breath and added in a small tight voice, "But I have given you my oath, and you can use me as you please."

Startled, the dragon raised up on one elbow the better to study me. His hand traced a line down my belly. I trembled and bit my lip to hold back a cry.

"Are you afraid of me, Red Bird Singing?" I hesitated, then nodded. He smiled, showing his teeth – not a sight to reassure me. He ran his hand across my belly again. "I will never abuse you like the vermin I killed," he told me softly. "I am many things, but that kind of cruelty is not in my nature. If you want me to stop now, I will."

Did I want him to stop – really? If I said yes, he likely would keep his word and comply with my wish. And if he stopped and never touched me again, would I be missing a priceless experience in the bargain? Coupling with one of the Goddess's avatars, what would it be like, exciting, dangerous? I felt like a gambler shaking the dice. I considered for a moment longer, then said, "No. Don't stop now. I want you to continue. I'm sure it will be different with you."

"Different with me, eh? Yes, our coupling will definitely be different – for both of us." The dragon's deep laugh came again, and he ran his long, brown tongue across one of my nipples, teasing it erect.

I shivered. This time he knew it wasn't from the cold. He smiled, then licked the ruddy bud again. "It doesn't matter to me if you are a virgin or not. And as for our lack of experience with this kind of pleasure – well, we will have just that much more delight in exploring the possibilities, hmm?"

Yes, I decided, we would.

Don't miss out!

Visit the website below and you can sign up to receive emails whenever Celu Amberstone publishes a new book. There's no charge and no obligation.

https://books2read.com/r/B-A-YGQM-NXTSB

BOOKS 2 READ

Connecting independent readers to independent writers.

Did you love *Refugees and Other Stories*? Then you should read *The Dream-Chosen*[1] by Celu Amberstone!

[2]

Humans and aliens struggle to survive on a planet surface foreign to them both, which still suffers the aftermath of a past disaster. Dunnagh is responsible for his people, wanting to bring his soldiers and civilians to safety. The Khutani work to preserve not only their own people, but the races of this planet Timorna where they dwell. It takes all the Khutani mind powers, and those of Dunnagh, to bring them together for symbiosis.

The Dream-Chosen is the first book in the series Tales of the Kashallans, by celebrated author Celu Amberstone. Drawing on her Indigenous and Celtic heritage, Amberstone writes powerful fiction subtly different from the usual science fiction or fantasy adventures. For fans of the 'Hundred Worlds' approach used in *Star Trek* and in Golden Age magazines, there are diverse settings and cultures along the journey taken by these human and alien characters.

---

1. https://books2read.com/u/m2lRA6

2. https://books2read.com/u/m2lRA6

"I never say no to writing by Celu Amberstone!" -author Joy Sanchez-Taylor

"I can't tell you how refreshing and original this opening chapter strikes me. Not only do we begin to understand the premise of the book and the mindset of the Khutani, we also learn, in a visceral way, how truly alien they are. Brilliant... Definitely makes you want to read more.

"Okay, three races involving an unusual biological relationship, hints of treachery and betrayal, hints of past and future disasters, moderately advanced technology, highly advanced psy powers, magic and spiritual power taken for granted, and a galaxy-wide environment. This is space opera writ large combined with both fantasy and hard SF. That's one heck of an accomplishment to establish in two short opening chapters. Even without knowing there are multiple volumes, it's obvious the ***Tales of the Kashallans*** *constitute a genuine epic written with such skill that you will be enthralled however long the series lasts.*

"This is a richly detailed fantasy/space opera that is positively addictive. Celu Amberstone has the knack of weaving elaboration and action into a vivid tapestry of action and character. Well rounded, deftly written, and a joy to read. Highly recommended. Consider it a useful antidote to mundane life these days... a genuine pleasure you owe yourself." -R. Graeme Cameron for ***Amazing Stories***.Amberstone's world-building puts together brave new peoples and gritty adventures, evoking strong responses in the reader. - author Paula Johanson

Also by Celu Amberstone

Rituals

Blessings of the Blood: A Book of Menstrual Lore and Rituals for Women

Deepening the Power: Community Ritual and Sacred Theatre

Tales of Tasimu

Taste of Memory

When Memory Dies

Abandoning Memory

Tales of the Kashallans

The Dream-Chosen

The Hunted Kashallan

The Outlawed Bond

Uncertain Refuge

Prey of the Umwira

Blood Magic's Snare

Kashallan Alliance

Treacherous Campaign

Standalone

Refugees and Other Stories

About the Author

Celu is of mixed Cherokee and Scots-Irish ancestry. Celu Amberstone was one of the few young people in her family to take an interest in learning Traditional Native crafts and medicine ways. This interest made several of the older members of her family very happy while annoying others.

Legally blind since birth, she has defied her limitations and spent much of her life avoiding cities. Moving to Canada after falling in love with a Métis-Cree man from Manitoba, she has lived in the rain forests of the west coast, a tepee in the desert and a small village in Canada's arctic. Along the way she also managed to acquire a BA in cultural anthropology and an MA in health education. Celu loves telling stories and reading. She lives in Victoria British Columbia near her grown children and grandchildren.

About the Publisher

Kashallan Press is an independent publisher releasing books by author Celu Amberstone. Among her books are critically-acclaimed works now re-released by Kashallan Press, and new works showcasing her talents in writing both fiction and non-fiction.

www.ingramcontent.com/pod-product-compliance
Lightning Source LLC
Chambersburg PA
CBHW051917240626
47153CB00004B/1260